I0635583

PRAISE FOR KAT & STONE BASTION

No Weddings and
THE NO WEDDINGS SERIES

"One of the best romantic comedies of the year!"

AGENTS OF ROMANCE

"The No Weddings series is one of the best I have read that follows one couple. Cade and Hannah are both lovable characters, the storyline is real and entertaining, and the banter is fun and witty."

LIVES & BREATHES BOOK BLOG

"I loved it, and I mean REALLY loved it!"

ORCHARD BOOK CLUB

"This is an exceptional series... You find yourself fully engrossed in their world and can't put the book down."

BOOKS -N- KISSES

"The No Weddings series has a group of such amazing characters; you can't help but relate to them and feel the emotion in every situation they encounter. It has been a long time since a story has made me feel that way let alone an entire series!"

UNDER THE COVERS BOOK BLOG

"The story of Cade & Hannah's relationship is realistic, heart-warming, and filled with real-world connections that shook me in a way that few titles I've read this year have managed...I have loved every minute of the No Weddings series."

THAT'S WHAT I'M TALKING ABOUT

Heartbreaker

"This book has definitely earned its five stars and I am just floored right now. The passion is explosive, the story itself is beautiful, and the emotions are so real my heart is ready to burst. Beautiful book. Absolutely breathtaking."

ONE PAGE AT A TIME

"Heartrending, passionate, and captivating! *Heartbreaker* is a riveting page-turner that will leave you breathless with raw emotions, and the need to hold tight to the ones you love!"

BENEATH THE COVERS BLOG

ALSO BY KAT & STONE BASTION

No Weddings Series

No Weddings · One Funeral

Two Bar Mitzvahs · Three Christmases

For Valentine's

Unbreakable Series

Heartbreaker · Rule Breaker · Lawbreaker

Forthcoming: *Ball Breaker · Icebreaker*

Comic Book Date Series

The Accidental May the 4th Comic Book Date

The Unbelievable Made on a Dare Comic Book Date

The Irresistible 4th of July Comic Book Date

Standalone Novels & Novelettes

Brand New Year · The Espionage Effect

Highland Legends Series

Forged in Dreams and Magick · Bound by Wish and Mistletoe

Born of Mist and Legend · Found in Flame and Moonlight

THE TRAVELER: Initiate Years

Veil of Realms · Secrets of Alexandria · Panther Rising

Stones of Power · Highland Magick

Romantic Poetry for Charity

Utterly Loved

"This book is all about flawless writing, exemplary storytelling, f*#king insane character development. The right dose of sexy hotness..."

LOVE N. BOOKS

"The Bastions are at it again with this beautiful and heartbreaking story. You will absolutely fall in love with Kiki and Darren's love."

UNDER THE COVERS BOOK BLOG

"*Heartbreaker* is a phenomenal story."

THAT'S WHAT I'M TALKING ABOUT

"I loved it...wonderfully compelling, a story that touched my heart in so many ways and characters I will remember for a long time to come."

GIRL WHO READS

Forged in Dreams and Magick

First Place – Unpublished Beacon Award
Best Paranormal Romance

First Place – Hold Me, Thrill Me Award
Best Paranormal Romance

Chosen by FreshFiction.com as their Fresh Pick for October 22, 2013

"A beautifully woven tale about love, choices, courage and destiny, *Forged in Dreams and Magick* is one of the best time-traveling novels. Fans of Gabaldon's *Outlander* will love it."

BOOKISH TEMPTATIONS

"I was gripping my iPad like a crazy woman and fanning myself from the smoldering romance. Lawdy!"

THE FLIRTY READER

"Bastion's debut is pure perfection, a combination of romance, magic, emotion, adventure and surprising twists and turns. This is a truly unique romance that should not be missed!"

THEBOOKQUEEN

"HOLY HELL!!! I am so... um... wow! FABULOUSNESS. *Forged in Dreams and Magick* definitely makes my BEST OF list for 2013..."

THAT'S WHAT I'M TALKING ABOUT

"A story guaranteed to enthrall with lushly detailed travels into times long gone by. Woven with love, passion, magic and legend, the story had me hooked from the very first chapter."

READ-LOVE-BLOG

"Kat Bastion's wonderful debut brings a new voice to the fore. Her voice is strong and unhesitating, very human and real, sometimes young and delicious in her treatment of intimacy and relationship development."

FANGS WANDS & FAIRYDUST

"OMG, Bastion hits all cylinders in this supernatural tale. The layers in the book were fascinating, and I devoured the fun, adventuresome read."

LITERATI LITERATURE LOVERS

Bound by Wish and Mistletoe

"I LOVED it! *Bound by Wish and Mistletoe* is, to my mind, a perfect entry in the historical / paranormal fiction genre and has quite a bit to offer."

FAB FANTASY FICTION

"Kat Bastion has done it again! ... Excellent holiday novella, perfect for a cup of cocoa and snuggling under a blanket in front of the fireplace this holiday season."

THAT'S WHAT I'M TALKING ABOUT

"Move over, Julia Quinn and Sabrina Jeffries! Kat Bastion is an absolutely gifted author and deserves to be recognized for her talent."

LOVESHISTORICAL BOOK REVIEWS

HALF-BAKED HOLIDAYS

HALF-BAKED HOLIDAYS

A ROMANTIC COMEDY HOLIDAY COLLECTION

KAT BASTION

Half-baked Holidays: A Romantic Comedy Holiday Collection is a collection of fiction. Names, characters, places, occurrences, and theories are the products of the authors' imaginations or are used fictitiously. Any resemblance to persons, living or dead, locales, events, or theories is wholly coincidental.

The authors acknowledge the trademark status and trademark owners of products, names, and/or phrases mentioned within this work of fiction, which have been used without permission. The publication of the trademarks is not authorized by, associated with, or sponsored by the trademark owners.

Half-baked Holidays: A Romantic Comedy Holiday Collection

COPYRIGHT © 2021 Kat Bastion

All rights reserved

Except by a book reviewer, who may quote brief passages for the specific purpose of reviewing this book, no part of this book may be reproduced, copied, stored, scanned, transmitted, or distributed in any form or by any means, including but not limited to mechanical, printed, or electronic form, without prior written permission of the authors. Please do not participate in or encourage piracy of copyrighted materials in violation of the authors' rights. To reach the authors, please visit either their blog at https://talktotheshoe.com or their website at www.katbastion.com and complete the contact form on Kat & Stone's Connections page.

Cover and layout copyright © 2021 Kat Bastion

Cover art copyright © JackyBrown/DepositPhotos

ISBN: 9781957025018

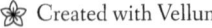 Created with Vellum

INTRODUCTION

Why write a romantic comedy holiday collection, you wonder?

Well, first of all, if you asked me what my favorite holiday is, the answer would be easy.

And complicated.

Because with absolute certainty, I most adore Christmas *and* New Year's Eve.

Why the duality?

Both vibrate with the magic of romance. In equal measure.

Exquisite and addictive. Exciting and heartwarming. Brimming with wonder and hope.

And if we're lucky, that incredible magic enchants us, entwines itself around us, and never lets us go.

The most wonderful time of the year definitely spun its powerful magic on us: Stone and I were married the day after Christmas.

We sent out elegant iridescent red-white-and-green poinsettia wedding invitations.

Had a small ceremony (Stone refused to shake the hand of someone he didn't know).

Annnd... the hip-hop beats of Run-DMC's "Christmas in Hollis" streamed on a tiny black boombox.

At the wedding.

Not kidding.

So with off-kilter humor deeply entrenched in our own holiday romance, it's easy to see why we believe romantic comedy deserves VIP seating at the holiday romance event.

And of course, there's no shortage of tasty ingredients...

All the delectable seasonal trappings: nostalgic songs, festive food and drink, sparkling decorations, ribbon-tied wrappings, and bright fluffy snow.

But dig a little deeper, and we also find all kinds of scrumptious emotion. Tender hope. Grumbly defiance. Aching love.

Whip into the recipe a pinch of humor and a dash of attitude?

And we all get to have... *Half-baked Holidays.*

Delicious chaos as romance and yuletide collide.

Five brand-new multicultural romantic comedies, written specifically for this collection:

Family chaos erupts as former high school crushes toss mischief into their first Christmas in... ***So NOT a Silent Night***

A sweet volunteer bedecks herself in Christmas trimmings to lure a dreamy firefighter in... ***Enticing Wrapper Number 9***

A Wharton MBAer ditches her trying family for a spontaneous Hawaiian yoga instructor in... ***Give Me a Christmas Break***

Two daring college students engage in breaking and entering—a personal baking contest—in... ***Half-baked Holiday***

When besties con their way into the ultimate party, a law student finds herself caught in... ***Billionaire Bash New Year's Crash***

Read on to adventure into the romantic merriment for yourself.

With great pleasure, I introduce you to... *Half-baked Holidays*.

I hope you enjoy the heartwarming romances.

Kat Bastion

SO NOT A SILENT NIGHT

ONE

THE BRISK DECEMBER cold penetrated every one of the layers Amanda wore. She stood outside the family home. At the crack of dawn, Christmas Eve.

The family home.

Not *her* family home.

Yet family apparently occupied the giant two-story house.

Her new enormous blended family. More than half of which she had yet to meet.

The other half? She didn't know. Not really.

For that, she blamed Oxford. And a million other things.

Not the least of which had been anger. And fear.

Shivering from more than the bitter cold, she clutched a Starbucks holiday drink with both hands like a liquid life preserver. Its lovely heat warmed her fingers. The festive cup wore patterned red-and-green horizontal stripes, mimicking a Christmas sweater. But touching the white lid to her lips, she sipped what mattered most—before eight a.m. on meet-the-family-day—caffeinated sugar. A quad-shotted Sugar Cookie Almond Milk Latte, to be exact.

Rich coffee, laced with sugar and spice, danced over her tongue. A small comfort.

But set adrift at Christmas, she'd take whatever bits of control she could steal.

Taking several hard gulps, she glared at the cheery house. At the red front door's shiny brass knocker, surrounded by a fluffy green wreath with fat red ribbons and big silver balls. At crisp white horizontal siding. The large paned windows trimmed by bright green shutters. And two pristine white columns, supporting a curving upstairs balcony, striped by diagonal wide red ribbons to mimick candy canes. Plus a gray shingled roof, dripping with strands of icicle lights.

Perfect. A house straight out of a fairy tale story.

And she stood outside, on the cold gray sidewalk. The stranger. A traveler from afar.

Another mouthful of the sugary latte went down her throat on a hard swallow.

The first rays of the sun set fire to a crystal-encrusted snowfield, beginning to wash away all the twilight gray. Illuminated holiday art sprawled over the yard: a variety of iced gingerbread playhouses. Glittered light over a forest of candy canes, gardens of colorful lollipops, and flowerbeds of shimmering wrapped treats.

Every child's dreamland.

Well, every child except her.

Movement caught her attention in one of the upper windows. An adorable small head had appeared with a halo of curly brown hair. Pale brown complexion. Cherub face. Bright smile. Little hands plastered to the pane. Nose tipped onto the glass.

Feeling ridiculous, stalking out there on the sidewalk, she took a step backward. Down off the curb.

Then she turned toward the black economy rental car—away from the child, from the house—doubt churning in her gut.

You're such an idiot.

For trusting them. Believing in the fairy tale. Getting her hopes up by imagining what a family could be. *Her* family... if she only gave it a chance.

But she had believed before.

And had been deeply disappointed.

More than once.

Halfway down the car's short length, she stopped. She pinched her eyes closed.

"You've come all this way," she muttered in argument.

And she had nowhere to go.

No real excuse not to walk the path. To be brave. See what unfolded. Come what may.

Which meant she needed to prepare for the inevitable letdown.

Unless...

Give me an out. Any out. And I'll take it.

Not that she was afraid... much.

Only that she listened to the universe... more.

A sudden rhythmic clicking sounded from behind her, growing louder.

She glanced over her shoulder.

A bright red truck with noisy studded snow tires approached, then slowed as it passed. It hooked a left into a driveway, across the street, two houses down.

The driver's door opened and a man got out. Then he stared her way.

He left the truck door open, walked down the driveway, then stepped into the street, heading toward her.

Slushy ice on the pavement crunched under his black snow boots.

The man looked a little familiar. Dark skinned with thick black brows, high cheekbones under crinkling eyes, and a strong jawline with a trimmed goatee. Handsome.

Dressed in a black wool peacoat. Black leather gloves on his hands. Charcoal tweed herringbone flat cap on his head.

As he neared conversational distance, he shook his head, a half-smile stretching full lips. "Amanda? Amanda Cobb?"

Delicious bass tones flowed through her, warming her insides.

Just like it had in high school. A lifetime ago.

"Why, *Trey Holloway*. As I live and breathe."

Breathing a whole lot easier, blowing out a relieved exhale through pursed lips.

Because the universe had just granted her a gift: her teenage crush.

"What are you doing here?" he asked.

"Good question." One she had no answer for.

"Visiting?" His brows twitched up a little.

She glanced back at the cheery perfect house. Then shrugged. "Don't know yet."

He glanced at the house. Toward the upstairs window. Where a second cherub face had appeared. The new one a little older, maybe three or four. Lighter skinned. With darker hair. Now four little hands pressed to the window, two kids staring down at them. Two noses pressed to the glass.

Trey arrowed an assessing look at her. Heavy. Searching.

Which made him all the more handsome. The man who'd been little more than a boy all those years ago, but had been her whole world back then. Star running back of the football team. Charming guy who'd mentored her on the debate team. Senior to her sophomore. Before he'd gotten drafted by the NFL, after graduation, and gone on to play the pros.

He cocked his head a bit, mirth creasing the corners of dark eyes. Older and wiser eyes. "You hungry?"

"Famished." Sad plane food on the redeye had only been picked at. "But... I probably shouldn't leave that there." She dropped a nod toward the rental car, which she'd naively parked in the center of the giant house's side-walk. "Makes it look like I committed."

He stared at the car a beat, then quirked a brow at her. "Unlocked?"

She reached into her coat pocket and pressed the key. The car chirped. "Yep."

He opened the driver's door, slid halfway in, gripped the wheel, and pressed a button.

The car coasted forward a few yards, his left boot skimming the icy road. When he passed a snow-dusted boundary hedge between neighboring properties, red brake lights flashed, then went dark.

"There. Now no one knows where it belongs." He got out, then shoved the door closed.

"Great," she muttered.

Pretty much summed her up in a nutshell.

TWO

TREY COULDN'T BELIEVE his luck.

Seconds after he'd grumbled about needing to find a woman with a kind heart, there she appeared. As if dropped from the sky.

And not just any woman.

The woman.

The captivating kindhearted girl from his past. Cast from his dreams.

Who'd been *way* too young for him then. When a whirlwind of incredible opportunities had swept him away.

But, *now*...

Oh, my. Amanda had grown into something else. Had become a breathtaking woman. Dark glossy hair falling in waves past her shoulders. Pale skin blushing a gorgeous pink in the cold. Inquisitive vivid blue eyes hiding behind thick dark lashes.

And those full rosy lips...

She licked them as she glanced at him. Making the lower pouty one shine. Showing her nervousness.

He ached to lean down and kiss her. Distract her into

forgetting every senseless worry. Worries that spun in her overactive mind and weighed on her generous heart. Like always.

The ache to kiss her burned, from deep inside his heart. Same as all those years ago.

The attraction then? Instant. And hard. Frustratingly hard.

But now... Magnify that tenfold.

It felt as if no time had passed.

They'd chatted random small talk the last few minutes, down the street, to his open truck door, then on up to the house.

Now there she stood, larger than life beside him, on the front stoop. Shoulder to shoulder, her lime-green puffer jacket brushing his coat. Wearing faded blue jeans and white zippered puff boots. While hugging a red-and-green Starbucks coffee cup in bare hands.

And she smelled incredible. Sweet, with a hint of spice. Like a Christmas cookie.

The brown grocery bag in his right arm crinkled when he shifted it, gaining a better grip on the paper through his glove.

The fifteen-degree temps were cutting through his coat and gloves. Had to be affecting those bare hands, no matter how warm the coffee.

Time to dive in.

"Ready?" Ready for his family.

Because after her look of dread toward the big house across the street—filled with a football team of kids—he knew she needed to get her feet wet. Meet a small amount of chaos.

Then maybe she could handle the big leagues. And whatever daunting fears she faced.

Peals of laughter ripped out, from behind the green-painted door in front of them.

"Whose place is this?" she asked as he reached for the brass doorhandle.

"My sister's. And her hellions."

Slender dark brows arched, doubt flashing across her face. She mouthed *Hellions?* while stepping inside as he held open the door.

The rich smell of fresh-brewed coffee hit him in the face. Along with the mouthwatering scent of bacon.

Which all masked the nasty burnt-pancake stink. Their round-one experiment, from earlier that morning. Packed into his grocery bag? More ingredients. For a modified pancake experiment: Round Two.

Some kids program blared on the TV in the family room up ahead, high-pitched voices extolling the virtue of sharing in singsong.

"Want more coffee?" He closed the door, glancing with uncertainty at her cup.

"Yes, please." She waggled the cup, signaling she'd gone empty.

With the cozy warmth of the house already seeping into their bones, she unzipped her jacket, then shrugged out of it, revealing a nubby white turtleneck sweater.

Which clung to incredible curves.

A flash of arousal speared through him.

In his *sister's* house. With her four little kids somewhere close by.

Mind out of the gutter, Holloway.

He gave himself a mental headshake.

Plenty more things to focus on. Like hoping even a small dose of chaos didn't scare her off.

Surprised the entryway hadn't already erupted into a

frenzy, he set the grocery bag down for a moment on the console table. He stowed his gloves, then hung their coats and his hat on empty wall hooks.

A tangle of all sizes of boots lined the baseboard under the console.

He toed his boots off while she removed hers. Then they stepped onto the radiant warmth of the slate tiles in their thick socks.

A flash of kids blurred by in a tight mob.

Aha! There *it is.*

The hellions raced from the front playroom, through the family room, toward the kitchen.

Then the second littlest, ever observant about her world, edged back around the corner. "Uncle Trey!"

"That's Zoe." With her frizzy halo of blondish hair around her brown chubby face.

Another one burst back around the corner, stopping beside her little sis. "Uncle Trey!"

"And Clarisse." Whose wavy hair had darkened to light brown by her four years of age.

Two more hellions appeared. The youngest, with his darkest head-hugging fuzz. And the oldest at almost five, with two fat dark braids dangling to her shoulders, each tied with red and green curling ribbons.

"Brendan and Bailey."

The foursome stayed rooted in place. Side by side on the Berber carpet. Gawking wide-eyed at Amanda.

"Hurry up, Trey!" his sis called from the kitchen. "Griddle's sizzlin'!"

"You heard her." He growled at the kids, arching a bear claw toward them as he stomped forward.

Ear-piercing screams followed as the kids fled, racing off left again.

"Hey, Jasmine." When he rounded the corner, his sis dropped spoonfuls of pancake batter onto a griddle.

"Hey, yourself." She focused on batter dropping. "Start fillin' bowls. The kids are drivin' me nuts."

"This is Amanda. A friend of mine." Friend? Overly tame. But all he could say. At the moment. "From way back, in high school."

"Oh." Jasmine glanced over her shoulder with surprise. "Hey, Amanda. Welcome to the pandemonium."

"Hi, Jasmine," Amanda said, then turned toward the lineup of still-gawking kids. "Hello, Zoe, Clarisse, Brendan, and Bailey." She waved at the troop.

"Hi 'manda," said Clarisse.

"'Manda!" mimicked little Brendan.

"Wanna see our new puppy?" asked Bailey.

Trey put the bag on the counter and began unloading the list of demanded goods.

"A puppy?" Amanda arched her brows at the kids.

They vibrated with eagerness, wanting to impress her. He understood the feeling.

"Yep," Clarisse said. "Uncle Trey brought him this mornin'."

"In a green p'sent!" Zoe clapped her hands, blondish halo bobbing.

"With a big red bow," Bailey added.

"That *wiggled*." Clarisse hunched down, then shook her booty in imitation.

All the kids burst into high-pitched giggles.

"Mommy? Can we *pleeease*?" begged Bailey.

"*After* breakfast." Then Jasmine pegged Trey with a stern look. "*While* uncle Trey supervises. And *cleans up* after the puppy."

Amusement sparked over Amanda's expression. "Not housebroken?"

"Wigglin' wasn't the only thing comin' outta that present." Jasmine fought a smile, then began flipping pancakes.

"Worth it." To bring joy into a household in dire need of it.

He glanced at Amanda.

And maybe joy might be headed for a couple more wayward souls.

He hoped.

THREE

FIVE MINUTES LATER—AFTER changing the blaring television to a Christmas coffeehouse channel streaming old holiday standards (per Jasmine's request)—Amanda settled beside Trey at a large trestle dining table with the rest of the energetic tribe.

Zoe, Clarisse, and Bailey had climbed onto the bench across from her.

Brendan occupied a high chair at the opposite end. And Jasmine anchored the corner of Amanda's bench, breaking up plain pancakes into baby bite-sized pieces.

The whole lot, filled with warmth and curiosity, had already won her heart with their gigantic eyes and broad smiles.

And Jasmine's house wrapped around her like a home, with its warm hardwood floors, brightly colored slip-covered furniture, and general laidback vibe.

Their dining room was wedged into the elbow corner between the kitchen and the family room. On the far wall of the family room, a fieldstone fireplace took up most of the wall, its orange flames crackling behind a botanical iron grate.

From a chunky wood mantel dangled six stockings. Two big reds, JASMINE and TREY in red block letters stiched on their white fringed tops. And four small whites, red sequins on their white tops scripting the children's names.

In the back corner towered a ten-foot tree. Trimmed with so much garland, tinsel, ribbon, and ornaments—in silvers, reds, greens, and whites—that the only clue a tree existed under it all was the monstrosity's conical shape. A lit LED star at the top shifted color every few seconds, rotating through the hues of the rainbow.

On her way back from her channel-changing assignment, she'd noticed the reason for Jasmine's single-mom thing. A silver-framed photo of a family of six took up a prominent position on that mantel above the stockings. With a happy Dad in a navy military uniform. Pale complected. Round freckled cheeks. Huge toothy smile. Cradled in one of his arms, a tiny baby slept, swaddled in blue blankets, not more than a few weeks old.

Alongside the photos, to its left, stood another frame. A gold-framed shadow box with black velvety matting. Which proudly displayed two golden medallions: a purple heart, hanging from a purple ribbon and a silver star, dangling from red-and-white stripes.

A distant echo of poignant sadness had pinged through her heart at the sight. Because she'd experienced that loss too.

Yet she shook off the memory. Hers had happened a million years ago.

No stocking had been hung for their Dad. Probably done with serious thought and intention. So as not to confuse the kids.

And with Brendan about fourteen months, and the tribe seeming reasonably adjusted without Dad, Amanda figured the loss of their father had to have happened shortly after Brendan's birth.

Not that any amount of time filled that gaping hole.

Sitting at the breakfast table with them now, she smiled at a beautiful family in the midst of celebrating. And vowed to focus on that elevated emotion. The infectious joy of the present moment.

She lifted a giant Santa-head mug to her lips, cupping the jolly face with both hands. Enjoying a hot refill of the caffeinated stuff. Straight black and fully leaded, for her second dose of the day.

Because with the breakfast-crazy slowly unfolding on everyone's plates?

No added sugar required.

She put her mug down on the trestle table, then gaped at the odd bowls of toppings. "What *in the world* are we doing to these pancakes?"

"Decorating them," replied eldest Bailey, all matter-of-fact, while scooping a spoon through a bowl of rainbow sprinkles.

"Like cookies!" Clarisse plunged a small fist into the decorating bowl nearest her, filled to the brim with flat candy dots in reds, whites, and greens. The bowl over-flowed, tiny candies splashing out.

"Gummies!" Zoe leaned forward and planted two tinier hands into a bowl translucent red and green gummy trees. Scattering more candies about.

"Right." Amanda shot a dubious glance at Trey.

Then she followed Bailey's more refined example (unsure where the tots' hands had been, with the puppy and all) and dipped a clean spoon into the so-far pristine rainbow sprinkles.

The kids smooshed their fistfuls of candies into the tops of their pancakes. Which already soaked up a lake of maple syrup.

"No sugar highs here." Like she had room to talk, with her glucose-charged Starbucks Sugar Cookie latte.

"Only on holidays." Trey arched his brows at the three-some. "Right kids?"

"*Yay* for *holidaaays*!" Bailey shot both hands into the air. Raining candy bits onto her neatly braided hair.

So much for the refined child.

The younger two mumbled unintelligible replies, around mouthfuls of candied pancake.

Jasmine arrowed a knowing glance at Amanda. "Makes for a perfect naptime crash."

The adult plates had no syrup lakes. Only a couple of respectable pancakes, a pile of scrambled eggs, and a few strips of bacon: her plate three, Trey's five.

Amanda slathered butter onto her pancakes, drizzled on a modest amount of maple syrup, and forked off a piece. Then she daintily rolled her syruped bite in her rainbow sprinkle cache—which sat in a carved-out well of scrambled eggs—like any civilized person. Then she popped the candied bite into her mouth.

Over the next fifteen minutes, she ate like that with the joyful zany tribe. A tightknit family who hadn't thought twice about her unexpected arrival. Who had—to the last child and adult—treated her as one of their own.

The little ones chatted with her nonstop, whenever their mouths weren't full of food. Offered her more candies, when her plate ran low. Asked which candy, of all the candies in the *whole wide world* were her favorites.

"Dark chocolate hazelnut truffles," she replied.

Which resulted in three blank stares.

And they shared detailed stories of their *most* exciting adventures. Including, and most especially, the new puppy.

Baby Brendan cooed and clapped, pacified by a never-ending train of pancake bites and entertained by his jovial trio of sisters.

"Sooo... you're visiting, from out of town?" Jasmine asked, guessing.

"Moving back to the states, actually. Straight from Oxford."

Trey straightened beside her at that tidbit. His thigh had been pressed against hers, the whole time they'd been eating. Which had been nice. Intimate.

He'd been mostly silent during the pancake feast. Letting his nieces hog the conversation.

"*Are* you visiting?" he arched a brow at her. "Committed to the idea?"

He referred to car he'd moved, to camouflage her arrival. The big house across the street. And the enormous family of strangers inside of it.

Yet after the warm reception of his smaller tribe, anything seemed possible. The welcoming visit, with him by her side, and his incredible lovable crew, bolstered her courage.

"Yeah, I think I am."

To commit.

Maybe in more ways than one.

And maybe... not alone.

FOUR

MOMENTS AGO, as soon as the grownups had stopped eating, while the girls still played with their food, Trey slid his hand against Amanda's. Over her jeans-clad thigh. Under the table.

And to his relief, she hadn't reacted to the contact.

Had shown no surprise at all.

Instead, her hand had slid under his, then rotated, till they were palm to palm.

Soft fingertips had traveled, in gentle exploration, along his skin. Stretched up the length of his fingers. Then in a slow flexing and clasping move, they entwined their fingers, together.

Excitement vibrated through him. Over holding hands. Charged about taking the chance. Thrilled that she'd accepted.

He buzzed on a crazy high. Like some virgin high schooler.

Cool by him.

He felt dialed back in time. With another chance at an amazing girl.

Except both of them thrown way forward, into a much better circumstance.

Both old enough. Wiser. Ready.

For something serious. Which Amanda had always deserved.

Karen Carpenter's soulful "I'll be home for Christmas" streamed from the TV behind them. "...although I *knooow*, it's a long road *baaack*..."

The table looked like a candy-shop explosion, a disaster zone of rainbow sprinkles, sugar dots, and gummy trees.

Colored smears stained the girls' lips, cheeks, and hands.

For half a second, as the kids repeatedly plunged sticky hands into candy bowls, he'd worried Amanda might freak over the unsanitary mayhem.

But she hadn't flinched. Not once.

In fact, the more the kids had laughed and played, chatting her up—while Jasmine hand-fed Brendan, taking it all in stride—the more relaxed Amanda had grown. All the tension rolling off of her, from when she'd been standing on the street, looking conflicted, had gradually faded away. Over the course of one very unorthodox breakfast.

Brendan began to fuss, done with his meal and being strapped into the high chair.

Jasmine wiped his face with the washcloth on his tray, then stood from the end of the bench.

And with that all-clear signal, the girls sprang from their seats and raced out of the dining room, through the family room, and out of sight.

"Wash your face and hands!" Jasmine ordered.

But seconds later, too fast for any washing to have occurred, tiny barks sounded, from the opened laundry room.

"*That puppy*." Jasmine stared at the ceiling and sighed.

Trey shot Amanda a mischievous glance.

The corners of Amanda's lips twitched.

He chuckled and gave her hand a gentle squeeze.

Then he stood and began to stack the dirty plates.

Amanda huffed out a silent laugh, standing and starting to help.

Jasmine shooed them both away with waving hands. "*Go*. Play with the girls. I've got this." But then, she turned back around, glancing at Amanda. "Will you be around later tonight? Any interest in Christmas Mass at St. John's?"

"Ummm…" Amanda glanced at Trey, then arched her shoulders. "Maybe. If I can… I'd love to."

He leveled a hard gaze at her. "I hope so."

She needed to know how deep he had fallen.

And he didn't want their reunion to end. Not so soon.

Maybe not ever.

The deep level of that sudden commitment shocked him.

But he'd known Amanda well, once upon a time. They'd shared some heavy stuff back in the day. Had practiced debates for the team with the topics of her troubles—at her request. Couched around childhood abandonment. Absentee parents. The nuances of responsibility, legal and moral.

She'd also been one of the hardest working members of the debate team, training for their competitions. Fearless, in a way. More so than any other member. Including him.

He'd believed back then that she funneled all of her heartache and passion into those moments. Gained control where she could. Craved the undivided attention from her teammates. Their reliance on her. And their expressed gratitude.

And whoa, had she bloomed under their adoration and praise. A delicate rose unfurling under its first nourishing rays of the sun.

Turning away from the kitchen, he hadn't taken two full steps before Amanda slid her hand back into his.

Right as the girls bounded into the room, a small black-and-tan German shepherd puppy chasing their feet.

"Trey?" Amanda tugged his hand, stared up into his eyes.

"Yeah?" He sighed, wanting to kiss her again.

Squeals and laughter surrounded them.

But he waited. Willing to be patient. However long it took. Ready for things to be perfect, on this unexpected second chance of theirs.

"Would you mind... I mean, would you want to..." Her brows twitched downward.

She struggled. With doubts. About way too many things.

Things he could help with. Ease her troubles.

Just like he had all those years ago.

But this time... so much better.

"Yes." He read her like an open book.

"Yes?" She turned her chin a fraction, tilting her head, narrowing her eyes. Confused.

Adorable.

He gave her hand a reassuring squeeze. "Yes, I'd love to go over to your house."

FIVE

AMANDA STOOD in front of the big cheery house's red front door, Trey by her side.

She had reached into the center of that fluffy wreath, with its fat red ribbons and big silver balls, and rapped the brass door knocker three times.

But she'd done so with thick knit mittens on. Charcoal, with tiny light gray double-stacked *V's*. Knit by crafty Swedes.

But courtesy of Trey's nieces. After he had made a plea to the troops to properly accessorize her for winter.

After which, a pile of mittens and scarves had gotten dumped on the living room floor. Most in sizes for little littles. Two pair had been donated from Jasmine's stockpile. Which were the only ones that fit. And Jasmine had insisted on Amanda taking a pair. As her Christmas gift.

The girls had insisted on a couple of other things of theirs though.

Snugged onto her head? Bailey's donated Santa hat. With head band and ball in fuzzy tan-and-black leopard print. And around her neck, they'd wound a sparkly red-

and-green garland scarf. Which itched and scratched wherever it touched her neck.

But after she had zipped up the collar of her puffer, she
tugged the scarf down, to a manageable jacket-insulated
level.

All the accessories reminded her of the special kind of
love found inside a real home. Each one a memento of a
family of six that she'd gained over breakfast.

Gave her the courage and desire to try her luck across
the street. Discover the possibilities behind front door
number two.

Bags crinkled beside her. Trey adjusting gloved grips on
the handles of the brown shopping bags they'd retrieved
from her rental car's trunk.

She glanced up at him. Licked her lips in nervousness.
Sweetness laced the tip of her tongue. Remnants of their
wonderful cookie-pancake extravaganza.

Dark eyes, shining with warmth, searched hers. Then
he gave her a nod.

She stared at the red front door again. Behind the
wreath.

Sounds of muffled chaos filtered through. Screams and
squeals. Laughter and shouting. Barking. Growling. From
children? Wailing. Whining. Covered by peals of laughter
again.

A real family. In all its crazy glory.

She took a deep breath, squared her shoulders, then poked
the corner of her mittened hand onto the doorbell button. The
only thing with a chance at penetrating through the noise.

They waited.

Long seconds later, when the cacophony continued
without pause, after it became clear that no one could

possibly hear their attempts at contact, she reached for the doorhandle.

She depressed the latch and pushed. Finally ready to meet everyone. Come what may.

The door gave way, swinging into a large tiled entry, littered with a dozen pairs of boots.

Decadent scents teased her next breath. Roasting meat, maybe. Onions and garlic. Savory, rich, and tangy, bringing to mind sweet potatoes and berry pies.

The muffled soundtracks of more than one movie boomed their bass tones. From above?

Panicked at intruding unannounced, she swallowed hard and closed the door.

A wide entry hall had two white square-cased openings, each leading to a larger room, one on each side. Farther ahead to the right, four wide green-carpeted steps curved up to a landing, then a narrow staircase climbed on up, back-dropped by pink-yellow-and-green floral wallpaper. Beside the stairs on the ground floor, beyond a wooden console table flanked on either side by velvety green armless chairs, a narrower doorway led to a corridor which contained several shadowy doorways.

Red bows trimmed the spindles of the staircase.

But the open space ahead in the hall, dead center on the hardwood floor, captured her concerned attention.

She held her breath, uncertain how to proceed.

Because they had walked in... before an immediate silent audience.

Straight in front of them stood a gaggle of six international knee-highs. Who all wore footy pajamas, some red-patterned, some blue. And every single little little stared wide-eyed at the obvious intruders.

"Hi, guys." Amanda waved a friendly Swedish mitten at the group, praying no one broke out in screams of alarm.

"Playing Star Wars?" Trey asked, noting light sabers—almost bigger than the kids—were clutched two-handed by three of the boys.

Bright smiles broke out.

One of the older littles, a darling round-faced Asian boy, took two steps forward. "Hi. I'm Kwan."

She grinned wide, sighing in relief. "Nice to meet you Kwan."

Four older youngsters, twin boys and two girls, bounded in a tight pack down the staircase, dressed in jeans and long-sleeved Disney T-shirts in various Christmas graphics. They paused at the lower landing, all staring her and Trey's way.

An older girl, about ten years old, wandered in from the larger room off right, face downturned, focusing on a thick hardback book she held in both hands. She wore her dark hair in one long braid down her back. Black-framed glasses were perched low on her nose.

At the sudden silence in the hall, the girl glanced up from her book.

Her gaze swept past Trey, then landed on Amanda.

"Hey, sis." Spoken so nonchalant. As if Amanda had been there all the girl's life.

"Heyyy…" Amanda flushed with embarrassment. She'd blanked on her sister's name. Maybe she had tried too hard to forget, all those years ago.

The girl arched an imperial brow. "*Nicole*."

Right. Nicole. Clipped out with a bite of well-deserved attitude.

"Hi, Nicole." She flashed her an apologetic smile. "This is my friend, Trey." She hiked a thumb at him.

Trey gave a slight nod.

Nicole stared at him a beat, before glancing at the gawking audience.

Then the girl heaved out a sigh, snapped her book closed with loud thump, and rolled her eyes.

"Guess I'm supposed to introduce you," Nicole grumped.

A thrill raced through Amanda.

From the girl's fiery spirit.

With the knowledge of who she was, the baby sister she'd had to leave behind.

And how Nicole had grown. Who'd she'd become so far. In spite of her challenging environment.

"You know who she reminds me of?" Trey murmured, staring at Nicole.

"Yeah..." Amanda admitted. "*Me.*"

SIX

AFTER THEY'D SHUCKED ALL their outerwear in the front hall, after being invited into the family room by Nicole (who'd already disappeared into the room), Trey followed Amanda, carrying a large brown bag of presents in each hand. Behind an entire football team of young kids who raced ahead of them.

From somewhere upstairs, the vibrating bass tones of two different movies turned off, one, then the other. Seconds later, Bing Crosby began crooning "White Christmas."

A fireplace spanned the back wall. With a long mantel. And fourteen red stockings hanging from it. Only a handful of large ones. Most of them smaller. One of the larger stockings had AMANDA in red felt letters on its top white cuff.

In the corner stood a large Christmas tree. Strung with popcorn and cranberries. Decorated with homemade ornaments, lots of clay shapes and felted objects with sequins. Lit by multicolored blinking lights.

Trey had never been inside the house. Nor met the kids. But he'd seen the children countless times. Running wild across the yards, theirs and many neighbors'. The older kids riding bikes down the street. Younger ones playing tag and other yard games.

Some of the youngsters had come over to Jasmine's. To play with the girls.

But only at Jasmine's. Never across the street.

Because the two households' parenting styles differed. Wildly.

Jasmine's supervision didn't remotely approach helicopter parenting. But it remained a far cry from the football team's hands-off parenting.

Watchful eye won out over blind eye, every day of the week.

But the football team all appeared healthy, though. Happy. Well adjusted.

On the surface, anyway.

Same as Amanda, back in the day.

"You okay?" He stared at her as they took a seat on the couch, dropping the bags at his feet.

"Yeah." She stared up at him, tone soft with wonder. As if how she felt being there, after all those years apart, surprised her.

Authoritative Nicole—with big blue eyes (like Amanda's) peering through black square-rimmed glasses—waited until every sibling had lined up in a row, tallest to smallest, as she'd directed.

They looked like an obedient row of soldiers. At attention. Ready for inspection.

"Guys, this is our oldest sister, Amanda." Nicole slid her glance toward him. "And her friend, Trey."

Amanda clasped his hand. Then clutched tight.

He gave a gentle squeeze, glancing at her. "You got this," he murmured.

The vise grip on his hand eased, and she turned toward him. Those beautiful vivid blue eyes gazed at him. With gratitude.

No place he'd rather be. By her side. While she braved her new world.

"Amanda, this is your family," Nicole said.

"The twins are Greg and Dillon." The girl gave a nod at the tallest boys.

"Greg..." Amanda released Trey's hand, got up from the couch, and walked to the head of the line. She shook the boy's hand. "Dillon..."

Amanda went down the line, shaking every child's hand, acknowledging them individually.

In turn, each child beamed with excitement, as if they'd been waiting for this moment. Looking forward to meeting their estranged much-older sister.

Trey couldn't be prouder. How far Amanda had come, how much she'd grown.

"That's Ashley," Nicole pointed at the tallest girl.

"Ashley." Amanda gave the young girl a nod, shook her hand.

"Tiffany," Nicole said with a nod.

"Tiffany." Amanda smiled at the two girls. Both dark haired and light complected. Resembling the twin boys.

Nicole edged closer to the little ones. "Kwan was adopted from China."

"Nice to meet you again, Kwan." Amanda shook his hand.

The boy giggled.

"Pei Ling, too," Nicole added.

"Hi, Pei Ling." The shy little girl kept her hands clutched to her sides, so Amanda gave her a warm smile and bowed her head.

In quick succession, Nicole introduced the youngest four. Arunny and Kolab, smiling sisters adopted from Cambodia, who stared at Amanda with big dark eyes as each shook her hand. And Elvin and Mateo, short square-framed brothers from Guatemala, who held on to one another with both hands while Amanda affectionately ruffled the black hair on their heads.

Amanda turned, then faced the eldest. "And beautiful Nicole. I'm so sorry I haven't kept in touch."

Her sister's blue eyes blinked behind her black glasses. Sparkling with tears.

"S'okay," Nicole said with a half-shrug.

"No. It wasn't. But..."—Amanda stepped closer to her, opening her arms—"thank you for inviting me. Thank you for not forgetting me. Or giving up on me."

Nicole's lower lip quivered. Tears began to stream down her face, and she lunged into Amanda's embrace.

Amanda hugged her tight. Tears falling down her cheeks too.

After a few seconds, the line of soldiers broke rank. The littlest ones wrapped their arms around Nicole's legs. The rest piled in. Surrounding Nicole and Amanda. Linking arms in a group hug, while taking great care to protect the little littles.

Amanda did her best to hug them back. And in an instant, the two sister's tears turned into laughter.

Then the whole football team joined in with the giggles.

"Oh!" Amanda wiped her face, blinking away the last few teardrops. "I've brought presents."

"Presents!" shouted the older half of the crew.

The little ones just looked around, wide-eyed.

"Over here." Amanda gestured a curving arm for them to follow and returned to the couch.

Trey held open the two bags at his feet.

Amanda dug in with both hands. "Help me pass them out," she said, eyes bright.

The packages were all wrapped in white paper with a red Fair Isle design, a snowflake, tree, and reindeer pattern. The shapes of the gifts were long and slender. All identical.

Each child accepted their present, with a polite *Thank you*, then walked away to find their own private place around the room.

The last gift was handed to Nicole. "Thanks," she said, then sat on the couch, beside Amanda.

Loud ripping, crinkling, and tearing commenced a split second later.

Giggles rose around the room as the children held up or shook their present. A thin long object, one end bobbing with motion.

"I brought them over from England." Amanda scanned the room, watching their delighted faces.

Trey stared at one of the gifts, trying to make it out. "What are they?"

Amanda beamed, nudging a shoulder into him. "Queen's Guard bobbleheads."

He leaned over, murmuring into her ear. *"Brilliant."*

Then he put an arm around her and kissed the top of her ear, providing his support.

Because the football team of kids had been the easy part.

The hardest part? Yet to come.

He glanced down into the bags. At their empty bottoms. "No presents for anyone else?"

"Nope." Amanda stood from the couch. "My presence will have to be good enough."

SEVEN

BRENDA LEE SANG "ROCKIN' Around the Christmas Tree" on some upstairs sound system as Amanda wandered past a wood-paneled formal dining room and into a spacious sunny kitchen.

The bright décor had a cozy family vibe. White quartz counters with flecks of silver and pale blue atop white painted cabinets. Stainless appliances, the large refrigerator covered in crayon drawings. Colorful ceramic cookie jars shaped like Snoopy and Woodstock.

Four yellow barstools sat tucked under a breakfast bar at a large kitchen island. On the end of the island's matching quartz counter sat three cooling pies: apple, cherry, and pumpkin.

An iron baker's rack against the wall stored all manner of glasses, bowls, and plates. Along with stacks of green linen napkins and red placemats.

A sizable round wood table with six white spindled farmhouse chairs occupied a bright corner, its large windows overlooking a back courtyard, facing southwest.

Snow-covered at the moment. Probably a pretty patch of garden come summer.

In the formal dining room that she'd passed had been a large rectangular table. With fourteen chairs. Enough for everyone. At once.

They all got to sit down and eat with a giant family. Together.

A man she'd never met before stood at the stove, back toward her, shaking seasoning over a large blue ceramic frying pan while sautéeing with a green silicone spatula. He had a broad build and a full head of silver hair.

In front of a white apron sink stood a woman, bent over the left side, scrubbing down into a tall stainless stockpot. Silver streaks ran through the woman's short dark curls.

The kitchen had a palpable energy within its walls. The perfect room to enjoy family. A great space for all those kids to get fed. Feel loved.

So different than what Amanda had experienced. Standing alone in a tiny galley kitchen. Learning to make Kraft macaroni and cheese. So she didn't starve.

The woman at the sink rinsed the stockpot under running water, stuck it upside down on a drying rack, then turned.

A peaceful expression lent the woman uncommon beauty. Almost a decade had aged her. But not much. A few lines bracketed her lips. But at forty-two, she was looked young.

They locked gazes.

"Hi, Mom." Amanda leaned a shoulder against the doorjamb.

"Oh, *Mandy*." Her blue eyes brightened. "I'm so glad you could make it."

"Me too." Hard to lie about that. Not after Trey's family

breakfast. Not after the eleven incredible kids she'd met in the living room. Wanting to be loved. Like every child does.

And to be fair, her mother had done her best. She'd gotten pregnant her senior year in high school. Married her father, who'd joined the military to earn a living. Only he'd gone off to war and never made it back.

Her sister Nicole had come much later, when Amanda was fifteen. Through a short-lived second marriage.

The other four older kids? From a third marriage, after Amanda had flown the coop.

The man at the stove had turned. Watched the two of them with trepidation.

Her mom walked over to the man, who put his arm around her. "Mandy, this is Roger."

"Nice to meet you, Roger." Total truth. Because somehow this last marriage had stuck. Good for her mom, some stability. Great for the legion of kids they had their hands full raising.

Kind gray eyes held her gaze. "Happy you could make it, Amanda."

"Need any help?" *Please say no.* Awkward didn't begin to describe how she felt. A stranger in foreign territory.

"No." Her mom glanced up at Roger, clear happiness in her eyes. "We've got this."

Roger gave her a nod. "We'll be ready for lunch in about an hour."

Cool. An hour to cause some mischief.

Become the kid she'd never gotten a chance to be.

TURNED out an hour wasn't nearly enough time for a proper amount of mischief.

Because all the kids had taken that entire time to introduce Amanda and Trey to every animal housed under the roof. And several out back.

All while she and Trey held hands. Like a brand-new couple. PG-style.

Greg and Dillon showed off their two creepy spiky green iguanas.

Ashley and Tiffany, a cute pair of brown teddy bear hamsters, running around in the same cage. That due to no babies, they'd decided were both girls. Two boys hadn't even crossed their minds.

Kwan housed a sweet little box tortoise named Ralph in a wooden habitat under his bead.

And Pei Ling kept a blue parakeet named Sky in a cage beside hers.

Arunny and Kolab had gotten littermate kittens, as an early Christmas present the day before, both black fuzzy cutie-pies with green eyes.

Inside a large terrarium, Elvin cared for three red-sided garter snakes. They had vivid red heads, black bodies, and bright red dots running between blue stripes head to tail.

In a more alarming development, Mateo pulled off the tattered lid of a flimsy shoebox to show off his fuzzy black tarantula.

Then finally, taking them out into the backyard, to a doghouse under the shelter of a patio cover, Nicole introduced them to Hero, an adorable older English bulldog.

After that? Lunch seemed... uneventful.

Especially following the breakfast-crazy with Trey's family.

The menu? Simple.

Spaghetti with meatballs. Garden salad. Garlic bread. Bowls and a platter with each ran down the middle of the long table, three at one end, three at the other, a third set in the middle.

The kids didn't mind the basics. They dug in, happy to be fed.

The large dining room had two crystal chandeliers, one at each end of the table. Plus a big south-facing window that streamed in daylight.

A buffet against the wall held a golden menorah on the left side, with nine white unlit candles. On the right, a small flocked Christmas tree. Undecorated, with no lights.

Interesting. She'd grown up with Santa Claus. And church... on holidays.

Then again, the family had become multicultural with the addition of Roger.

Maybe they had also gone omnireligious.

But she didn't ask. Didn't care, really. Whatever made them happy.

Which... seemed to be the case.

Mom asked about plans after graduation. Roger asked if she'd found a job.

Amanda shrugged to both. She hadn't decided. And hadn't looked.

Her brothers and sisters peppered her with the rest of the questions. *What was England like?* "Sunny and rainy." *Did she get to fly the plane?* "No! But how cool would that be?" *How many brothers and sisters did she have over there?* "Five hundred and forty-three."

Amanda worked to keep a serious expression on that last one.

But with all the wide-eyed shocked faces staring back at her, she burst out laughing.

"*None.*" She swept a glance across every one of their beautiful faces. "*You* are my only brothers and sisters. And I'm incredibly grateful to finally meet you."

Nicole served as manners monitor, making sure they all were polite, and all took turns.

And Trey and she held hands again, under the table, just like before.

Which filled her with a glowing warm happiness.

But toward the end of the meal, a slight commotion erupted.

All the kids ducked under the table.

When their mischievous faces popped back up, they all pounded their bobbleheads onto the table with a resonating boom. And eleven soldiers of the Queen's Guard bobbled their black fuzzy-hatted heads up and down.

Boisterous laughter broke out from everyone, adults and all.

"'Manda?" A slight double-tug pulled at her sweater sleeve. Little Pei Ling stared up at her, from the chair beside her. Had quietly climbed into that chair once Amanda had been seated.

"Yes, Pei Ling?" She stared down at her adorable new baby sister. One of the two who'd pressed their noses to the glass in the upstairs window. Arunny had been the littler one. Staring down when Amanda had hovered out there on the sidewalk at the crack of dawn. Indecisive about going up to the big house.

"I'm glad yo' my sis," Pei Ling said.

Warmth flooded her heart. A cramp choked the base of her throat.

"Me too, Pei Ling. Me too."

EIGHT

TREY HELD AMANDA'S HAND. More certain than ever. That he planned on never letting go.

Amanda frowned. "Sure this is okay?"

They'd stepped into his sister's church.

Yet with its wood-arched ceiling towering high above, central aisle stretching down wooden pews as long as an airport runway, and large stained glass windows depicting the stations of the cross, the cavernous hall skewed more toward a cathedral.

The singing choir way up at the elevated front, dressed in red robes, seemed tiny from the back where they'd entered. Or maybe that was the children's choir?

A giant Christmas tree glittered with silver and gold back in the corner, behind the choir. And rows of red poinsettias in shining green-foiled pots flanked either side of the front section.

A musty scent, old wood with a hint of sulfur, almost made him sneeze.

Blasting heat had him strip his coat off. Amanda ripped off her puffer even faster.

"No." He wasn't sure about anything else. Only of her and him. Not one other thing mattered. "But we're off rules tonight, right?"

"Right." She gave a determined nod.

What she'd decided after gaining her football team of a family. That she got to be a kid again. If only for one night of the year.

In the hours after lunch, they'd made a racket all through the house. The kids, most of all.

Two played trumpet. A third, drums. So they'd created a marching band.

No instrument? Spoons and pans worked just fine. And they marched and clanged and sang Christmas carols through every room in the house.

All afternoon.

But during dinner, which had been two turkeys with all the fixin's, Amanda mentioned she wanted to go to church with Trey's family.

Which resulted in Amanda's brothers and sisters all shouting they wanted to go too.

And so, storming the back of St. Johns, were Amanda and Trey, the hellions, and the football team.

Squeals and stomps, along with the pitter patter of tinier feet rushed down the aisles.

"Back here, girls," Jasmine called, herding her flock into their seats.

But Amanda's side of the family? Unsupervised.

Because Janice and Roger had stayed home.

And Amanda and Trey didn't care. Much. They were part of the rowdy crew.

None of the parishioners appeared alarmed. Maybe Christmas Eve mass always went a little unruly. On account of the à la carte holiday faithful, and all.

Amanda, Trey, and the rest of the football team filed in to the available rows. Not the last two rows, those had already been snagged. But the third and fourth to last, against the aisle. In front of his sister's family.

Mass started.

And in the hush of the sermon, the strangest noises came from the pews around them.

Tiny mewling noises, off toward his right.

A soft whimper. From right behind them?

Something fuzzy, tiny, and brown skittered into and down the aisle. Then a second fuzzy tiny something. The teddy bear hamsters.

Chased by two tiny black kittens.

Then a small black puppy.

An older woman screamed.

Amanda and Trey ducked down, hiding on their pews.

"What did you two do?" hissed Jasmine.

Trey glanced up at her sister's flashing dark eyes.

"Nothing," he muttered. *Much.*

He leaned into Amanda. "I *might* have told Arunny and Kolab the kittens could come."

Amanda smirked. "I *might* have told Ashley and Tiffany the hamsters could come."

"If they *stayed* in their coats," they both said.

"But who told the hellions?" she whispered.

Pride flared in his chest. "I think the girls bent that rule all on their own."

TREY STOOD with Amanda at the head of their street, in the darkness of night, but with dozens of yard light displays glowing and flashing.

They walked hand in hand down the center of the snow-dusted road. Jacket and coat zipped and buttoned. Leopard-print Santa hat and tweed herringbone cap snugged down. Woolen Swedish mitten clasped to black leather glove.

"I *CAN'T* BELIEVE we got kicked out of *church*." Amanda's breath fogged as she huffed out a laugh.

"Think we're blacklisted?" Trey asked.

"We better not be," Jasmine groused, edging in beside them. "That is *my* church."

But then Jasmine winked at Amanda and hurried after her girls.

Bailey held the puppy in her jacket, walking beside Nicole.

The rest of the kids raced from one light display to another or tromped through the snowy yards.

The older kids erupted into a snowball fight.

Little littles chased after one another.

He and Amanda kept a watchful eye on all of them. Occasionally picking up and righting any toddlers who stumbled.

"*Sooo...*" Trey gave her hand a squeeze. "Think you might want to stay in town?"

"If I got the right offer." She gave an innocent nod.

"I'm making the offer." He turned toward her.

"But..." She faced him, staring up, brow furrowing. "Aren't you a professional football player? Don't you live somewhere else? Or have to travel?"

He gave a solid headshake. "Mangled my knee two years in. Dropped out and went into sports medicine. I run a clinic a few miles away."

"Really?" She blinked at him.

"Yep." He tugged her forward again, so they could walk and talk, watching the kids. "Sooo...?"

"Stay in town." She flattened that down into a statement, as if confused.

"That's what I'm asking." He tried not to smile.

"You're making an offer." Doubt vibrated through the tone.

"Maybe one of the houses on this street? A big family of our own?"

She stopped walking, glanced up at him. "Trey Holloway, what kind of offer are you making?"

"Maybe an official date first? Then dat*ing*? Then..."

"A house and a big family." Her expression blanked, lips parting, breaths shallowing.

He shrugged, trying to diffuse the serious tension. "Only if you want."

She exhaled a heavy breath through pursed lips.

But then she tugged him close, leaned up, and pressed the softest tenderest kiss on his lips. A spectacular kiss. One he'd been waiting forever for.

He wrapped his arms around her, deepening their kiss on a sigh.

When they eased apart, pure joy sparkled in her darkened blue eyes.

"Yes, Trey. *Yes*. I *definitely* want."

EPILOGUE

THE FOLLOWING YEAR, on Christmas Eve, Amanda strolled down the street with Trey.

They'd walked hand in hand, having just walked over from their darling three-bedroom bungalow. From two streets over and halfway down that block.

Because it was cool and all to be close to the relatives.

But not *too* close.

She and her mom still had a strange distant relationship. Strained and awkward.

But they both connected, on a really deep level, with all eleven of Amanda's siblings.

All that mattered, in the end. And a great thing to have in common.

Night had fallen over the neighborhood, a pitch-dark moonless sky stretching overhead.

But the whole street had beefed up their Christmas light displays, better than the year before. Setting both sides of the street ablaze with glittering color.

Neighbors had blocked off the ends of the street with

cars. Turning it full-on pedestrian... for just the one night. Whether or not the law allowed it.

No one had asked. No one cared.

And tons of children played in yards piled high with snow. Adults too.

Squealing, shouting, laughing, screaming, little ones ran every which way, filled with the merry mayhem of Christmas.

One yard had a snowman contest, building snow guests who attended a holiday party.

Her family had expanded their gingerbread village, with stomped-down pathways curving every which way, for kids to run through.

Jasmine served hot cocoa from an end-of-the-driveway stand, a girlfriend from work helping pass out the steaming paper cups.

None of them had gone to church that night. No one dared risk another animal catastrophe.

But every pet remained indoors. The one and only rule of the night.

"Well, what do you think, Mr. Holloway? Happy we settled here?"

"I dunno." Arm around her, he pulled her tight against his side. "What do you think, Mrs. Holloway?"

Then he leaned down and kissed her. One of those amazing, breathtaking, knee-wobbling kisses of his.

A sweet little sound cooed up between them.

From the beautiful babe strapped to his chest, under the warmth of his coat.

Their teeny tiny little, Amelia. Bundled in multiple thermal layers of pastel red and green. With a thermal baby Santa hat warming her adorable little bald brown head.

"Yeah." Amanda leaned into Trey's side. "Beyond happy."

Willing to break grown-up rules, one night a year.

Working on building their own family, one precious soul at a time.

And so very blessed to have their giant extended families, kept close to their hearts, visited often. The hellions... and the entire football team.

ENTICING WRAPPER
NUMBER 9

ONE

HOPE COULDN'T BELIEVE she'd gotten so desperate. Fallen so low. That in the depths of loneliness, she'd resorted to wearing such a ridiculous outfit. Within the quaint subdued wrapping section. Inside the cavernous steel warehouse. Packed with hundreds of volunteers, all preparing for The Great Christmas Toy Drop.

Nonetheless, there she stood.

On Christmas Eve.

Gaudy as holiday hell.

Red-and-white striped stockinged feet crammed into green elf stilettos: candy cane heels, red satin side bows, jingle belled toes.

Green plaid miniskirt pinafore. Over a clingy cleavage-baring scooped-neck tee. Candy cane striped. Of course.

Luxurious custom-knit long Santa hat. A deep plush red. With fluffy white trim around her face. And a poufy white pom at the end. The whole stocking cap shaped like some inviting festive question mark... its big bottom dot resting above the swell of her right boob.

Yet apparently, the basic level of decking herself in holiday humiliation? Not enough.

Nope. Not nearly enough. Not to get noticed by the one hot guy of her fantasies—who couldn't be bothered to look up from his wrapping workstation.

No room for error. No time left to leave anything to chance.

So, for the pièce de résistance, she'd woven battery-powered LED lights into the Santa hat. From the fluffy white top trim to the poufy white pom.

God-awful *multicolored* lights.

That blinked.

A question-mark Santa hat turned beckoning neon sign, arrowing straight to her chest.

Clearly, she'd suffered from some kind of temporary holiday insanity.

Or possibly a severe blow to the head.

But out of options, in the last few minutes, of the eleventh hour, on the twelfth day of her Christmas, she squared her shoulders back, held her head high, and determined that she *would* get her dream man to notice her. Maybe not entice. Maybe not attract, even in a general sense. (Those ships had sailed with other subtler attempts, every other night that week.)

But at least that insufferable man would take notice.

The cozy workshop enclave had been tucked within the greater warehouse. Perimeter rimmed with green twelve-foot artificial trees, trimmed in tasteful solid white lights. Lining the inside of that festive forest, large wrapped presents stacked above her head, forming a sound-buffering wall. Concrete floors were draped in a red-white-and-green mosaic of overlapping tree skirts.

Outside their relative haven, obnoxious beeping marked

the backing up of a few of the dozens of forklifts that trundled unwrapped toys from one section to another. And between the beeping chorus, a cacophony of random conversations, directing shouts, and off-key carol singing hummed in the background.

The tens of thousands of collected unwrapped toys journeyed to their new home: transported through the makeshift assembly line, loaded into an assortment of converted delivery vehicles, to be deposited onto the doorsteps of less-fortunate children.

All the volunteers proudly represented frontliners across the valley. Assorted military branches. Various police personnel.

And, oh, *be still my beating heart...* firefighters.

Or rather, one firefighter in particular.

A sexy muscular quiet type.

Who seemed determined on focusing only on his task. And nothing else.

She stared down the aisle of wrapping workstations, four on the left and four on the right. Landed a harder stare at the lone desk behind them all, smack in the middle. Glared at the dark glossy black top of one stubborn down-focused head.

Wrapper Number 9: Miguel Rodriguez.

Thick black brows furrowed, as he concentrated on a fold.

Caramel skin clenched over a strong jaw, as he inhaled, nostrils flaring.

Taut forefingers creased a perfect seam, even with the Christmas-decorated plaster cast covering his right arm.

Incredible *large* fingers. Directed by that focused attention. Creating such nimble folds.

Heat flashed through her at the thought of what else he

might do with those fingers, with such focused attention, such precise dexterity...

Get a grip.

She blew out a frustrated breath.

One very long sexually frustrated breath.

Dignity stuffed somewhere down into her red pushup bra, she raised the silver serving platter, balanced on her open palm above her shoulder. Aromatic spices of its arranged gingerbread men—which she'd freshly baked—tickled her nose.

From speakers nestled somewhere in the perimeter trees, tense violin strains of "Carol of the Bells" played the soundtrack (of her fairy tale gone awry), rabbiting her pulse.

Her question-mark Santa hat blinked its multicolored lights in her peripheral vision, almost like a warning beacon.

Arctic air from an overhead exposed industrial vent blasted down, chilling skin gone damp with perspiration.

She swallowed hard.

Then she closed her eyes, gusted out another heavy sigh, and gave a slight shake to her head.

It's for the kids, *Hope.*

Not her sorry-ass dating attempt.

Ignore the sexy-as-sin fireman in the back.

Concentrate on your job. The one-and-only striper. Self-appointed to the group of nine wrappers, who operated under a severe time crunch. Amid the warehouse's hundreds of trackers, sorters, pickers, and stockers.

A striper. Long *I*, no double *P*. Self-named, with a nod to those candy striper volunteers at hospitals a bazillion years ago. Because that's where all the wrapped toys were destined in the wee hours that night and into the morning: children's hospitals and wards.

Self-appointed, because she'd arrived late (due to no

fault of her own) after all the jobs had already been assigned. The head foreman had explained the wrappers needed some kind of assistant support.

The twist on the assistance? She knew how to bake. So she delivered scrumptious Christmas treats to the hard-working wrappers. Home-baked themed cookies and tiny cakes. Cider and eggnog.

Served up with loads of holiday spirit.

Which she'd certainly outdone herself on tonight.

She sucked in a deep centering breath and opened her eyes.

With the slight lick of her lower lip, a bite of peppermint flashed across the tip of her tongue. From the frosty white lip-plumping gloss she'd shellacked on during her last break.

"*Walker!* You working or daydreaming?" Barked out from behind. Loud and jarring, from the head foreman.

Walker. Her last name. But her cheeks flamed at how the call-out sounded. How she felt. Primped and on display.

The icing on her humiliation cupcake.

But none of the nine wrappers glanced up. Decent of them.

"Working, sir." She gave a nod of her head.

Then she took a careful step forward.

But even with an attempt at smoothness in her gait, the large silver bells fastened to her toes jingled.

Miguel's head lifted a little.

He stared at an empty spot at the front edge of his metal workstation.

And she swore she caught the slightest twitch at the corners of his lips.

Of amusement.

TWO

MIGUEL KEPT HIS HEAD DOWN, refocused on wrapping the gift in front of him. Not just any kind of wrapping. Precision wrapping. Crisp folds. Smooth seams. Clean tape lines.

Even the odd-shaped boxes. Like the one in front of him. Which he'd become a master at.

In spite of the cast on his right arm, up to the elbow.

And the deep aches, straight down to the bones, with each flex and every press.

No matter *how badly* he wanted to look up from his task. Stare at the clear distraction. *Get* distracted.

Because a beautiful temptation taunted him: *Hope.* The girl who kept delivering cookies and cider. Who kept glancing his way... when she thought he couldn't tell.

Not that he planned to do anything about the enticement.

The last thing he needed? Complication. Not even something purely physical.

He let out a slow sigh, frustrated at what his life had been reduced to: wrapping presents.

Not fighting fires. What he'd been training to do for over six months. Except, he'd suffered from horrific luck. Had broken his arm the last week of fire academy.

Already on the fire department payroll, they'd given him essential chores and dull make-work. That had included his assignment to the toy drive.

Not that he was ungrateful.

After all, he'd been the dumbass in full gear who'd tried to stop a slamming metal door. With his forearm. From an awkward angle.

Stupid.

Which shoved the one thing he'd been working toward —looking forward to for years—on hold.

Which spiraled him down into the foulest mood. At the holidays.

Beyond The Grinch.

More like Ebenezer Scrooge. And then some.

Bah. Humbug.

Annoying Christmas tunes blared through speakers propped somewhere behind him. The music had just changed from some violin number to Mariah Carey's sappy "All I Want For Christmas Is You."

At the first notes, he glanced up. Unable to help himself.

Hope glanced down at the wrapper two stations ahead, on his left. Number Five. Jenson. An army guy. She handed him a brown cookie from an arrangement on a silver platter.

But Miguel's gaze snagged on something else.

Hope's outrageous outfit.

Crazy ridiculous. Totally sexy. And sweet... in a quirky holiday way.

As her head began to turn away from Jenson, body

twisting, Miguel ducked his head back down. Focused on taping the final seam.

Complicated.

Way more than a Grinchy Scrooge could handle. Or deserved.

A faint jingle of bells marked her position, without him looking.

But he didn't need to look. Had done plenty of that all night.

Jingle bells. On the toes of her shoes.

Stripper shoes.

The kind with three-inch platforms, on the green fronts, and seven-inch stilettos, all glittered up like candy canes, on the heels.

Sweet quiet Hope. *In stripper shoes.*

Miguel pressed his last tape strip down hard. Harder than his normal hard. Forcing that reliable ache to flare into both mending forearm bones.

Jingle. Jingle. Then a long pause.

She'd crossed the aisle. Delivered a cookie to Number Six, Moore, a female detective.

Hope's typical distribution pattern. From the top, his left, right, then down to the next row. Right, left, then next row. Left, right. Right, left.

Before she'd angle forward, dead center. To his workstation.

Saving the best for last. How he imagined it. The vibe he got from her.

Complicated.

He sucked in a deep breath, nostrils flaring.

The delicious scent of spiced gingerbread made his mouth water.

He raised his cast into the air. Signaled his stocker out in the warehouse to deliver the next toy to wrap.

Ten seconds later, jovial Vincent appeared. A fellow firefighter from a sister department across town. Heavyset balding older black guy. Gleaming white smile. Always a kind word or uplifting phrase. Next in line for station chief.

"Last one," Vincent said. He slid a gaming guitar onto the side of the metal worksurface. Then removed the soccer ball, wrapped expertly in red Peanuts holiday paper: Woodstock under a green knit hat, Snoopy wearing a red Santa hat and big white beard.

Vincent tucked the wrapped soccer ball under his arm, staring down the aisle. In Hope's direction. "Last chance"—he murmured, leaning closer—"to make a move."

Vincent had been ribbing him all week. Four days in, after Hope had deposited a tasty trio of iced rum balls on the plate at the corner of Miguel's workstation, he had gotten caught. Staring a beat too long at Hope's departing backside.

But, oh, what a *sweet* backside. Tight and round. Cradled by dark blue denim. Tucked under the cutest ugly sweater ever. Which had shamelessly featured the backside of a naked gingerbread man. Who held a red-ribboned wreath over his exposed gingerbread buns.

The scent of gingerbread in the here-and-now made Miguel huff out a head-clearing snort. "No chance," he repeated. Like he'd done every time with his cohort. "No moves to make."

Vincent shook his head, tsk-tsking disapproval. "Your loss, brother."

"Hi, Vincent!" Hope glanced up. Beaming a smile their way.

Miguel arrowed his attention back down to his workstation. Snapped a length of red wrapping paper out toward his left.

"Hi, Hope," Vincent replied, then glared down at Miguel. "*Make* the move. You're an *idiot* not to."

Yep. That about covered it. Idiot. With his arm. With his career.

But not with his decision to stay uncomplicated.

Smart. Safe. For all involved.

"Go stock toys." Anywhere else. Miguel folded the left side, then forcefully taped.

Vincent patted his shoulder. "You'll see. The best presents go to the kindhearted." He turned and shuffled away, muttering, "*Even* the blind and stubborn ones."

"No idea what you're talking about, old man."

Miguel wasn't blind. Or stubborn.

More like smart. Cautious.

And unwilling to get injured again.

Or hurt anyone else.

Except...

Those damned jingling stripper heels kept taunting him.

Dainty little steps down the aisle.

Jingle-jingle. Jingle-jingle.

Jingle all the way...

Staring down at the second fold of his guitar wrap, he gave a heavy blink.

Because while concentrating past Gene Autry's "Rudolph the Red Nosed Reindeer," he noticed a pattern change in those taunting jingles.

The dainty little footsteps had jingled right on past workstations seven and eight. She'd changed pattern. Headed straight toward him.

Pulse skyrocketing, he abandoned the wrap job. He

reached toward the left corner of his desk. Grabbed the mug —black, emblazoned in red with WRAPPER NO. 9— gifted to him his first day there by the foreman. He glugged down several lukewarm swallows of spiced cider—a beverage Hope had silently poured for him from a large carafe not thirty minutes prior.

"Hey, Miguel. I hope it's okay. I made this one just for you."

He gulped down two more hearty swallows of the spiked drink.

Shifting the tray lower, she grabbed a small red napkin from the side, then lifted the center gingerbread man.

She glanced down and took another step forward, lowering the cookie toward the empty white dessert plate on the corner of his workstation.

But as he caught sight of the gingerbread man, dressed like a shirtless firefighter—black iced boots and pants, red suspenders and helmet, water hose in hand—Hope's whole body vibrated with a tight jerk.

Panic flashed across her face.

Miguel shot up from his chair.

Hope flailed her arms, tray and two cookies tossed up in the air and flying backward, as her right leg crumpled.

Without thought, he dove.

Straight toward the sweet crazy girl he'd been doing his boy-scout best to ignore.

THREE

BODY HURTLING FORWARD, adrenaline racing, heat flashing hot across every square inch of her skin, Hope cast out a last wish to the Christmas gods to save her.

From serious injury.

From total humiliation.

From utter failure.

All caused by one vulnerable moment of loneliness-spiked insanity: deciding to wear super-cute elf stilettos. Higher than any shoe she'd ever worn—by several inches. One of which had caught on a tree-skirt seam, in the world's most embarrassing trip. Shooting her silver serving tray airborne. Launching the last two gingerbread men skyward. Threatening a face-crushing slam onto thin tree skirting that camouflaged unforgiving hard concrete.

Somehow, in those slow-motion seconds of disaster, she managed to twist, midfall.

The warehouse spun into a twirling kaleidoscope: colorful wall of stacked presents, green treetops strung with white lights, the horrified expressions of her small band of wrappers.

Pain speared through a clunked elbow. Then a banged knee. And ankle.

A hard thump vibrated into her head from behind.

Bright colors flashed.

Then... total blackout.

Except... not total knockout.

Because a helium-infused Alvin and the Chipmunks still trilled, "...*waaant* a plane that *looops* the loop... *Meee*, I want a *huuula hooop*..."

Right. She'd obviously hit her head. Hard.

"*Hope*." Spoken in a delicious bass tone. Sexy and warm. Murmured into her ear. From her dreamy fireman.

"Yes?" Breathy, raspy, even to her ears. But, hey. What the hell. Get knocked on the head? Suffer a fantasy delusion? *Not gonna argue.*

"You okay? Did you hurt anything?"

She frowned.

Sooo... not a fantasy?

Her head wobbled a little. As if, her landing pad... shifted?

She felt a slight tug on her hair, then the blackout disappeared. White fluff fringed her brows. Accented by multicolored blinking lights.

From the tacky Santa hat.

That had crawled over her face?

Great. Dignity gone.

Oh, but not as low as possible.

That fact became crystal clear as her vision focused. She stared in horror at the hem of her green plaid miniskirt, which had creeped all the way up to her hips. Flashing the whole wrapping department her red-and-white striped crotch.

Shoulders slumping in defeat, she stared down the

striped expanse of her legs, to her feet. One shoe on. The other sideways, jingle bells caught in the braided trim of a tree skirt. Both toes pointed straight up. Like the witch in *The Wizard of Oz*. The one who'd gotten crushed by a house.

But the only glittering ruby on her elf shoes were the candy cane stripes on the stilettos. Nothing magical about 'em. She didn't get to click the heels together. And her fairy tale didn't include *No place like home*. Because her home held no one waiting for her. No parents. No cousins or friends. No little dog Toto.

"Hope?"

With a deep inhale, nice and slow, the most wonderful scent teased through her nostrils. Spiced. Earthy. *Male*.

She swallowed hard, then scanned upward.

A plaster cast came into view, permanent markered with black-outlined green trees and red presents. Followed by the rich brown of a muscular biceps, which stretched the short sleeve of a charcoal tee.

Laughter bubbled out when her gaze landed on the tee's ironic graphic: a comic reindeer, antlers tangled in colored Christmas lights. Holiday humor she hadn't been able to see all night. What, with Miguel hunched low over every toy he wrapped. Like a caveman.

Come to think of it, he'd even grunted his appreciation of her treats. Every single night. Without ever saying another word.

The wobbling behind her head increased. Then firm probing pressed against her scalp. Through her Santa hat.

"I'm... fine." She lifted her head from his grasp. "No concussion." She didn't think.

Frowning at the rest of the wrapping department who'd gathered into a semicircle—staring down at her, worry etched into their expressions—she tried to get up. No need to have her candy cane striped crotch on display any longer than necessary.

When Miguel shifted with her, she twisted around to get a better view of what had happened. How he'd landed there, on the ground with her.

Then it dawned on her that the wobbling behind her head was because she'd smacked her head down on his hand. His *hand* had cushioned her fall. His *good* hand.

He knelt beside her, left denim-clad knee where her right shoulder had been.

"Oh my god!" She twisted further, leaning on her hip. "Your hand. Did I hurt you?"

Amusement lit up in his beautiful dark eyes. "Nah." He splayed then fisted his left hand. Rotated his wrist. "No serious damage done."

"You sure?" She reached out, took his hand into both of hers, then flipped it over to examine the back side. An angry red color blotched across the lowest knuckle of his middle finger and the tendons of his hand. "Maybe some ice?"

"Nope. I'm good." He tugged his hand out of her grasp, then arched his brows. "You?"

She rotated back around. She kicked off her remaining stiletto, then rolled both ankles. Only a slight twinge flashed in her left ankle, but no serious pain. "Nothing major. Only damaged pride."

The gawking wrappers relaxed their expressions and, one by one, turned way, dispersing back to their respective workstations.

Miguel began to stand, dipped a supportive hand under her elbow, then helped her up. He even began to tug the hem of her pinafore down over her hip. But when he moved to straighten her backside, she stepped out of reach, not comfortable with him fixing the mess she'd made of herself.

Concern drew his brows low as he stared at her.

Nervous about his silent focused attention—when he'd been focusing on everything *but* her for the last week and a half—she chewed on the corner of her lower lip.

A flash of peppermint, from the white lip-plumping gloss, reminded her that she'd *been trying* to get his undivided attention. Had been craving it for twelve long tossing-and-turning nights.

"Ummm... The night's almost over." Their last night together. Unless she dug deep, got brave, and finally went for it. "Maybe I could buy you a coffee?"

"No. I..." He glanced over his shoulder, at a half-wrapped upside-down guitar centered on his workstation, then back toward her. "I can't."

"No worries." She could take a hint. *Not interested.* Not after all the nights of subtle flirting, when she'd caught his eye, before he looked away. Not after dressing in the most *uni*gnorable holiday getup. And not after falling over him. Literally.

She shrugged, then blinked.

Tears pricked her eyes. A cramp choked the base of her throat.

She sucked in a deep breath and held it, spinning away from him. The last thing she wanted was for him to see the devastating humiliation she felt.

Bending over, she hooked a curving finger into each of her life-threatening elf shoes.

Then she began to walk back down the aisle.

The tossed silver platter already sat on the corner of Wrapper Seven's workstation. Seven and Eight had each placed a gingerbread cookie atop their plates. Helping her out. Not making a fuss about the spill. Or the embarrassing tumble.

She left the platter where it sat, since it had been lent to her by the toy drive organizers, and walked past.

The overhead speakers gave a fuzzy burst, interrupting Bing Crosby's "Do You Hear What I Hear?"

"Okay, folks. That's a wrap!" cheered a jubilant female voice. "Sleigh Stockers you're up! Get those vehicles loaded. Hospital Santas, you're on deck."

Yep. The announcement made it official.

Her time on their last night of volunteering had wound down to its end. Her job? Completed. Such as it was. The end of Christmas Eve, for the wrapping section, for the entire toy drive, had come.

She wasn't needed any longer.

Her shoulder's slumped again, head dipping in defeat, as she padded down the back half of the tree-skirt aisle in her stripy stocking feet.

And with high heels dangling from one hand, it felt like a bizarre walk of shame.

Walking away from the guy.

With none of the one-night-stand pleasure.

But a heaping amount of humiliation-pain.

FOUR

MIGUEL HEAVED OUT A SIGH, deep regret burning through his chest.

Hope's devastated expression etching into his brain.

Those sparkling tears in her eyes tugging at his heart.

The realization that he'd caused her such pain curdling in his gut.

He'd been a selfish jerk.

All because he couldn't get it together. Didn't want to take a chance. Refused to get complicated.

Idiot.

After the *That's a wrap!* announcement, Bing Crosby's "Do You Hear What I Hear?" crooned on.

Hope stepped from the tree-skirt floor coverings onto the bare concrete of the greater warehouse. And as she did so, her slumped shoulders lifted and pulled back, the blinking Santa hat raised, head held high, and she gave a little shake of her arms.

Jostling those adorable elf stripper shoes dangling from one hand.

Only, he couldn't hear the jingle bells from so far away.

Out she walked, her pride returned.

Out from The Great Christmas Toy Drop.

Out of his life. Forever.

Or... maybe not forever. He'd overheard her talking to Moore about being a new dispatcher. He could always track her down. Where, though? A police dispatcher? Or 9-1-1 operator? In Scottsdale? Or farther out, somewhere in the Metro Phoenix area?

Complicated.

If he couldn't accept a simple invitation—for *coffee* of all things—how in the world did he expect to follow through on tracking her down. And for what? That same coffee? Dinner? Something more...

Yep. *All* way too complicated.

She had no clue about his real attraction for her. If he'd only been honest with himself. Braver about everything. Willing to take the risk. For himself. For her.

He folded the wrapping paper over the back of the guitar. Taped down the seam.

Then he glanced up.

Hope's green-plaid form was smaller, then got hidden by a trundling forklift.

When the forklift cleared, she'd vanished.

Where shelving rows towered. Blocking the side exit of the warehouse.

Panic flashed through, burning that regret hotter in his chest.

That he'd never see her again. Her bright beautiful face. That wonderful quirky sense of humor. Pure goodness from the depths of her soul. Up to that zany blinking Santa hat. Down to those ridiculous stripper heels. Which had been *so opposite* of sweet adorable her. But her taking that daring leap of faith—wearing that quirky holiday costume, just for him (his possessive opinion)—definitely her. Through and through.

"Suck it up, Rodriguez," he muttered under his breath.

A healthy dose of courage obliterated the majority of the doubt.

"Don't be afraid of complicated."

In fact, if Hope meant complicated? He intended to embrace it.

No matter the outcome.

In spite of his worries.

Because something deep in his gut screamed that a possibility with Hope, whatever it might be... *worth the risk.* For both of them.

For the first time in twelve nights, he wrapped with speed, ditching finesse. Two quick folds over the top of the guitar's base. Another couple of sliding cuts with the scissors for its neck. Fold on one side. Fold on the other. Longer pieces of tape. Faster pressing of seams.

The kid would have to forgive the shoddy wrap job. Would probably be so excited to get a guitar, they'd tear through the paper anyway.

Kinda how he felt now. Excitement. Joy.

He raised his casted arm, signaling Vincent.

The exasperated look Vincent speared toward him, arms crossed over his barrel chest, shouted *About damn time!*

"Yeah, yeah," Miguel muttered. "I'm chasing after her."

He shot up, grabbed his personal items, then charged down the same aisle Hope had.

All while Crosby's parting line morphed in his mind...

She will bring you goodness and light.

He only hoped he hadn't blown it.

Hadn't come to his senses too late.

FIVE

NEW to more than just her job, after having flown across county to escape the slushy snow of Cleveland, Ohio, she had thoroughly researched and expected milder winters.

But milder was a relative term.

Daytime milder didn't cut the chill from nighttime temps.

Parking lot asphalt, well after ten at night, still shot cold through the bottoms of bare feet. Well, stockinged feet. But after padding slower, placing sore feet with tender care on the rough pebbled surface, holes and snags had to be forming.

The red-and-white stockings?

Ruined.

Right along with her dignity. Stuffed into the depths of that red pushup bra.

Hey, she'd given it a go. Had pulled out all the stops. Worn the sexiest craziest outfit she could think of.

But still, it hadn't been enough. What she'd thought all along.

At least, she'd tried.

Which had been a lot more than scaredy-cat caveman Miguel had done.

In those last moments, before her eyes had misted over, she'd caught the longing in his dark eyes. Along with a split second of indecision with a twitch of his brows.

But something held him back.

Something greater than an attraction she swore had been there, just under the surface.

Insurmountable, apparently.

As she picked her way across the parking lot, wishing she hadn't parked so far from the entrance, she thought she heard her shouted name.

She frowned. Muffled by the hum of traffic on the main road?

Impossible to hear. Right?

Right. She refused to turn around. She hadn't brought anything, besides the cookies, so she hadn't left anything behind. And didn't want some fragile naive hope shattered into a million pieces.

Even though the night was clear, only a few stars managed to sparkle through the dense metropolitan's lights. But the air had a crispness and relatively fresh scent. Something she'd take any day to dirty smog from back East.

After another few careful steps—gingerly placing the balls of her feet, then the heels, followed by the rest of her weight—another shoutout happened.

Clearer. Louder.

Her name. Without doubt.

Shouted in an unmistakable bass tone.

One that made her insides flutter.

She stopped, but still didn't turn. Because those frustrating tears welled in her eyes. Again.

"Hope." Spoken softer. From right behind her.

A gentle touch pressed at her elbow. The same elbow Miguel had supported. After her disastrous fall. Before the rejection.

The touch fell away. "Please turn around."

"Why?" croaked from a tightening throat.

"I was wrong."

"About?" She blinked the tears from her eyes, sprinkling them over her cheeks.

"Us."

"There's an us?" An annoying spear of hope flashed through her chest.

"If you give me another chance."

"Another chance." It felt like he'd had dozens of chances. Twelve whole nights worth. And yet, they'd both kept their attraction under wraps. Had been too afraid to take the leap.

But she *had* put herself out there. After making a fool out of herself.

Which had made the stark rejection all the more cutting.

"Ask me again." His deep tone softened further. Sounded closer. Silence followed, warmth pressing from behind, even though he didn't touch her again. "Please?" His tone elevated a tiny bit.

"No."

"No?" Disbelief lifted his tone a little more.

"Your turn. You ask now."

You be the brave one this time.

"Face me first." That sexy bass tone lowered again.

More commanding.

Dangerous.

Even so, she gave a firm nod, deciding to face him once more. "All right."

They'd stopped in a darker area of the parking lot. Between lampposts.

Which made the multicolored blinking lights haloing her face all the more pronounced. And perfect, actually. Brought lighthearted festiveness into the tension between them.

Then she turned.

His black hair was mussed. Spiky. Like he'd raked his hands through it.

"Will you hold this?" He held out his black mug.

Not the question she'd been expecting.

"Okaaay..." She took the mug with her free hand.

"Now, will you take a bite?"

She frowned. Even more confused.

He raised his other hand, holding out the gingerbread fireman. "I hope it's okay. You made this one just for me." She'd made it *as* him, actually.

He grabbed the cookie by the boots, extending the top toward her, till it hovered a few inches from her lips.

"You want me to bite your head off?"

"Yeah." He arched his brows. "Really wish you would. I deserve it."

Her lips twitched as she fought a smile. "Hard to argue there."

He lifted the gingerbread fireman closer, within biting distance.

Mug clutched in one hand, shoes dangling from the other, she leaned forward, then snapped off the gingerbread fireman's head with a hard chomp.

Then he took a massive bite, devouring the cookie's entire torso.

As she chewed her bite, the delight of melt-in-your-mouth crumbly cookie and holiday spices—nutmeg, cinnamon, and three kinds of ginger—exploded through her mouth. Strong heat from the ginger flared across her tongue and cheeks.

"Mmmm..." He groaned, eyes half-closing as he chewed his giant mouthful.

She watched, licking her lips, chasing the cookie with a taste of frosty peppermint, until his gingerbread euphoria subsided.

He swallowed, licked his lips, then stared down at her.

She arched her brows.

After a deep breath, he exhaled.

"Hope Walker, will you do me the great honor of having coffee with me?"

Her heart stuttered when he said her name, tone lowered with reverence over those three syllables. Made incredible when uttered from his lips. His expression grew eager. Vulnerable. Almost boy-like.

And yet, nothing else about him held that innocence.

The rest of the package? Amazing sexy man.

"Yes."

His face brightened. "Now?"

"*Where* are we going to find coffee so late on Christmas Eve?"

"I don't care." He half-turned and stuffed the legs of gingerbread-him down into his back jeans pocket. "We'll find somewhere. How 'bout your place? You got coffee?"

"Yeah. But..."

"No 'buts'." He stepped forward and crouched, then scooped her up in his arms.

She squealed with joy, as so many wonderful Miguel sensations surrounded her, his heat, his warm laughter, the spicy-earth manly scent of him.

At a sudden sucking hiss of his breath, she started in his

arms. Then she realized his casted arm bore the brunt of her weight.

"I can walk on my own." No way would she be party to harming him further.

He gave a hard headshake. "Not barefoot across the parking lot, you won't."

"What about a fireman's carry?" she blurted before she could stop herself.

Her face flamed at the image of that in her head.

He stared down at her. "You sure?"

"Every woman's fantasy?"

He cocked his head, doubt tugging at his expression. Then he raised his brows. "Okaay..." He placed her back down with great care.

Then he bent and tucked his left shoulder into her waist and hoisted her up, banding his left arm across the backs of her thighs.

"Okay?"

"Okay," she lied. Because while he strode off, all the blood rushed to her head.

And with every one of his steps, her weight lifted then settled, upper body thumping against him. Even when she relaxed. Especially when she tensed.

And no matter how she held the elf stilettos—lifted up, off to the side, or dangling straight down—they made quite the racket. Jingling all the way.

"Miguel?" She stared at the black asphalt, instead of the nice shape of his butt.

"Yeah?"

"Where are you taking me?" She hadn't told him where her car was parked.

"My truck."

"Oh." The asphalt brightened, then darkened again, as they passed under a light.

"That okay?"

"Depends. How far is it?" Because the fireman's carry had been fun. For half a millisecond.

"Just another few spaces."

"Okay, good." Because last thing she wanted to do, after her spectacular fall earlier, was pass out.

She'd been waiting twelve long sleepless nights for her firefighter to come around.

And she didn't want to miss a thing.

SIX

MIGUEL WAITED with the last unraveling threads of patience. While Hope struggled to fit her key into the lock. Three seconds later, she slid it home and turned it right, throwing the bolt.

They'd driven fifteen minutes from the warehouse, to her apartment building, perched at the corner of a freeway interchange. She'd explained the complex was all she could afford, after moving from Ohio, straight out of community college.

One year and a decent raise away from something better, she'd reasoned.

Not any different than my crash pad, he'd commiserated.

A place where he'd been living for two years. He'd gotten used to the traffic noise. And valued white noise machines.

Her covered parking space had a wide sidewalk beside it. Which she'd hopped out onto, before he'd even rounded the truck. Then she'd walked on her own from there. Right beside him. Christmas-lighted Santa hat blinking. His black mug clutched in one hand, tucked up against the red-and-white-striped tee at the top of her green dress, in front of her heart. Stripper heels dangling from the other hand, jingling with every step.

But once she pulled her key from the unlocked door, before she reached for the latch, he snatched her hand.

She turned toward him, glancing up in wide-eyed surprise. Big pale blue eyes. Fringed by dark thick lashes. Matched her beautiful thick brunette hair, hidden somewhere under that crazy Santa hat.

With a low growl, he dipped his head down, startling her even further.

Startling himself.

He needed to taste her. Needed to touch her. Regardless of where the rest of the night took them.

Luscious lips met his, soft and pliable. Tasting of peppermint. And gingerbread.

She leaned against him, rising up on tiptoe, wrapping her arms around his neck.

A double jingle sounded out behind him.

They both laughed softly into their incredible first kiss. A perfect kiss.

When they eased apart, she stared up at him, amusement sparkled in those baby blues. "Aren't you coming in?"

"Sure hope so." Not that he planned to take advantage. But he didn't want the night to end.

Her head tilted. Adorable confusion wrinkled her brow. "But... isn't it typical to kiss a woman at her door... at the *end* of a date."

"What about us has been typical?"

She licked her white-frosted lips. "Not much."

"Exactly."

A corner of her mouth quirked up. "Scared yet?"

"No way." *A little. Or... maybe a lot.* But not about her. "Intrigued."

"Good. Me too." She glanced at the door latch. "Ready for some coffee?"

"Ready."

"But I have to warn you," she said, opening her door, "The coffee sucks."

"The company is stunning. All that matters to me."

She beamed a megawatt smile at him. "*Great* answer." Then she swept an arm past her doorway with a hard jingle as she shook her shoes. "You have passed the test. You may now enter."

He gave a short nod, then strode into her apartment. Curious to learn more about her.

But with every next step, he realized *that* wasn't happening.

"Uhhh... *how* long ago did you move in?" She hadn't mentioned.

"Almost four weeks ago."

He stared at stacks of boxes, some open, most taped shut. At bare white walls. And a severe lack of furniture.

"Not in a hurry to settle in?"

She shrugged. "I unpacked essentials so far. Baking supplies..." She walked into the kitchen.

Where a tornado had touched down. Mixing bowls in all sizes cluttered both sides of a stainless steel sink. White flour dusted over a black microwave and stovetop. Over a tan counter scattered different kinds of "baking supplies." Whisks, spoons, spatulas. Molded cutting boards. Metal cooling racks.

"You unpack a coffeemaker?"

"Yup." She moved toward the far wall in the galley-style

kitchen. Where a silver and black machine rested. She put his black mug beside it.

Then she dropped her shoes. And they hit tan-patterned linoleum with a protesting jingle.

He ran through his mind what other essentials she could've unpacked. "Towels?"

She scooped coffee from a silver canister into the top of the drip machine. Poured water into its reservoir. "Hard to take a shower without one."

Annnd... hard to imagine *anything other* than her in a shower. Naked. Dripping wet.

He swallowed hard.

"Sheets, of course."

"Of course." His voice cracked, mind wandering there too.

Complicated. And happening. Risk. Reward.

Nervous, he wandered around the place.

"Living room," she said, following him as the coffeemaker sizzled, gurgled, and dripped behind them.

He snorted. "How do you know?"

She huffed out a laugh. "What?"

"No couch. No chair." Only boxes. And floorspace. And empty walls. With one window on the end.

She crossed her arms, glancing around the box-filled room. "No table or lamp, either."

"So how do you know?"

Her brows furrowed at the repeated question. "Who puts their bedroom off the kitchen?"

"Quirky people."

"Is that how you see me? Quirky?"

"Yes." Might as well admit it. "And *my* bedroom is off the kitchen." A studio apartment.

"Oh." She tilted her head again.

Then pleasure washed over her expression. At the sad things they had in common.

Yep. Her zaniness. What had finally done him in.

Her brows arched a little. "Want to see the bedroom?"

"Dunno. Will I recognize it? Does it have a bed?"

She shot him a glare. Then stuck out her tongue.

Which flared a piercing ache through his chest. Something he refused to label. *Complicated.*

A repeating beep in the kitchen waylaid the bedroom inspection. She darted back into the kitchen. But halfway back to the coffeemaker, she stopped in her tracks. "Oh, wait..."

From the stretch of counter opposite the stove, she tugged forward a half-open box, stuck her face down into it, and rooted around. She let out a sigh and a headshake, then moved onto another countertop box.

When she stared into the third box, he stood alongside her. "What are we looking for?"

"This." She pulled out a tall clear glass bottle with black-red-and-white labeling: the word PEPPERMINT over a red ribbon at the bottom. "Schnapps."

Five minutes later, they sat cross-legged on her bed, facing each other.

Well, on *half* a bed: a full mattress, on a box spring, on the floor, in the middle of her other room. Plain white diner mug in his hand, with a thick classic handle. His black toy-drop mug in hers.

The room was dark. Except for the Santa hat blinking over her brow. Which burst multicolored glows into the far shadows and onto her stark walls.

"This is now *mine*, by the way." She clutched the black mug with both hands. It's red WRAPPER NO. 9 facing him. She sipped from it, staring at him over the rim.

He gave her a slight nod. "My gift to you. Merry Christmas, Hope."

She swallowed down a larger gulp of coffee. Then her face brightened with joy.

"That's *right*. It's past midnight."

She surged up onto her knees, then inched closer, one knee at a time, mug held off to the side.

"Merry Christmas, Miguel," she murmured.

Soft lips molded over his. Tasting of coffee. And peppermint.

A deep kiss, full of promise.

Lots of complication. And so much more.

Something the quirky wonderful woman had brought into his life... goodness and light.

Hope.

EPILOGUE

THE FOLLOWING YEAR, Hope insisted they carry on their personal Christmas tradition.

On their first anniversary.

A second Great Christmas Toy Drop.

Fluffed around the wrapping enclave were the elegant green trees strung with simple white lights. Inside the perimeter, a stacked wall of wrapped presents, towering over her head.

Days one through eleven had gone by. Business as usual.

Both of them had worn jeans thus far. But they competed nightly with the other eight wrappers in a fierce ugly sweater contest. The other eight wrappers had all returned that next year, as well. A reunion of sorts. Everyone nostalgic about the camaraderie of their special division within the greater toy drive.

Hope still baked up a storm, trying out different cookies and cakes on her wrapping crew. She still provided hot beverages, challenging herself to mix new recipes. Spiked hot chocolates, mulled wines, twists on ciders and eggnogs.

And of course, Miguel kept his beloved workstation at the back. Maintaining his reputation as the odd-shaped-gift wrapper. And his designation.

Which she loved. The one and only: Wrapper Number 9.

But on the twelfth day of Christmas, on Christmas Eve, one year after she'd fallen for him, they changed things up. Just a little.

Both of them wore custom Santa hats, blinking with multicolored lights.

And he wore candy cane fireman pants, held up by red suspenders, over a tight green muscle tee.

She wore her same green plaid miniskirt pinafore. Over that same clingy scooped-neck candy cane tee.

But, *no stripper shoes*.

Miguel had been very firm on that point.

Those elf numbers were only for him. In the safety and privacy of their own bedroom.

A bedroom which was no longer at her place (two weeks into New Year's, they'd forfeited her security deposit.) But not at his old place either; he ended his month-to-month.

They'd shopped around and found a quieter apartment. A modern two-bedroom flat, tucked into a neighborhood that bordered a bustling shopping district.

Then they'd had a blast buying furnishings for their new place. Bold colorful wall hangings. A pale gray couch with turquoise throw pillows. And an actual bed, with a curved headboard in graywashed wood.

Yep. At the toy drive, her precarious stilettos had been nixed.

In their place, they'd decided on boots.

His and hers matching boots.

Stable-footed shiny red-patent-leather Doc Martens. With bright green laces.

And each boot had a trio of jingle bells fastened to the front.

Hope strutted down the aisle, stomping her jingle bells with every step.

Annie Lennox's rich contralto serenaded "Winter Wonderland" through the speakers.

Hope lifted a loaded silver tray high, intent on changing her serving pattern: back of the wrapper-brigade first.

Miguel hunched over at his station, shoulders curled in, brows drawn low, focused on some current wrap job. Must be quite a challenge. For the master wrapper to get stumped.

She stomped her boots harder.

But Miguel didn't lift his gaze. Nor his worried brow.

"What's got you stumped, babe?" She set the tray down, trying to see down into a mountain of tangled paper. "Anything peppermint fudge might help?"

His dark gaze met hers.

The corners of his mouth twitched.

He lifted up a twisted mass of wrapping paper. Every gaudy color and pattern represented. All the pieces had been shaped into thin tubes, their ribboned ends trimmed in paper fluffs. The conglomeration had been fashioned into some sort of crown. Or maybe a wrapping nest.

"Does peppermint fudge feel celebratory?" His brows twitched up a little.

"For our anniversary?" Their start had been ginger-bread. "Sure. Maybe fudge is a one-year treat."

"Or maybe *today* is ground zero." He lifted the twisted paper toward her.

"Ground zero?" She frowned, accepting the odd wrapping mass from him.

But then she saw it. A flash of sparkle in the very center of the nest. Fastened by a strand of green curling ribbon.

A sparkling round diamond solitaire.

With a startling jingle, Miguel launched up from his chair, then went down on one knee. He drew in a deep breath.

"Hope Abigail Walker, quirky holiday girl of my dreams, will you make me the luckiest caveman alive? Marry me?"

Warmth radiated through her. And gratitude.

That she'd taken an insane leap of faith one year ago. Dressed in a ridiculous outfit. Risked life and limb. And well-baked gingerbread men.

All for the sexy quiet type in the back.

Who was *just* as quirky as her.

"Miguel Santoro Rodriguez, offbeat fireman of my dreams, you make me the luckiest girl. Every day and night of my life. *Yes.* I *will* marry you."

Tears welled in her eyes. Happy ones, this time.

She collapsed down, aiming for his waiting arms.

But she clipped the silver serving tray perched on the corner of his workstation.

Squares of dark chocolate peppermint fudge rained down. Bits of red-and-white peppermint and tiny crumbles of fudge covered their blinking Santa hats and festive outfits.

They burst out laughing.

Miguel gave a firm nod. "The peppermint fudge has spoken."

"Yup." She fed him a square, while he lifted one for her. "Perfect engagement treat."

She took a dainty bite of hers.

Then she kissed him, luxuriating in the fudgy minty goodness of her perfect man.

GIVE ME A CHRISTMAS BREAK

ONE

"YOU'RE BLOCKING MY SUN," Brooke grumbled.

Expensive sun, cultivated through enormous effort. After trudging across chilly golden sand, alarmingly just past sunrise. Spinning the resort's lounge chair around, which turned her back to a glittering diamond ocean. Angling her position by the long shadow of her travel-fatigued self, to align with a red fireball of glaring light.

She'd raised the back of the blue-cushioned chaise one notch above flat, then collapsed down onto it.

Planted.

Exhausted.

Free… relatively.

She'd fled all things family at the crack of dawn. Found refuge in a few secluded chairs at the farthest edge of the resort. Past hedges with fragrant blooming white flowers that hid her location. Not the perfect spot, but the best she could do without a resort map. Or her own rental car.

Sans coffee. *Way* too early in the morning. On Christmas Eve.

Big round brand-new sunglasses perched over weary

eyes that had drifted closed. With slow determination, and no small amount of resignation, she inhaled the freshest air on earth. Doing her damnedest to absorb chill vibes, on the first morning of a forced two-week vacation.

Sunny Kona Coast, Big Island, Hawaii.

A million miles from Polar Vortex East Coast, Wharton, University of Pennsylvania.

And a bazillion miles from the incessant red-and-green jollity of Christmas.

Stuck in paradise, she surrendered to her circumstances, vowing to wipe the slate clean. Step off the emotional-turmoil treadmill. Absorb the laidback tropical atmosphere. With modest effort, she could even remake herself from the inside out. If not forever, at least for the moment.

Gentle waves lapped spongy perfect sand not far behind her, a soothing burbling rhythm. Farther out, breakers boomed, crashing against the black lava peninsulas sticking out above low tide.

Steady trade winds danced coolness over her bare arms, puffing open the short sleeves of her black peasant top, ruffling the airy pockets of her khaki linen cargo pants. Adequate gift shop finds from the night before.

A deep inhale through parted lips imparted a taste of sweet salty air.

She stretched her toes wide, the balls of her feet downward. Imagined the blazing sun as it scorched a straight-and-narrow path, up a blue cloudless sky, above swaying coconut palms. Considered stripping down to her new retro black-gingham bikini, to toast up some first tan lines.

Then she frowned.

Her skin hadn't begun to warm. The light behind her closed eyelids hadn't brightened.

The audacious shadow-thrower remained.

In her way.

"*Hey*." She propped a shielding hand at the top of her sunglasses. Squinted an eye open at whatever rude offender had the balls to harsh her mellow. "You're *blocking* my sun."

In the glaring light, all she could make out was a dark silhouette. Wide shoulders. A man. With something odd shaped on his head. Arm extended... connected to a vertical surfboard.

Great. A surfer.

"Maybe you need blocking." Sarcasm underscored a rich bass voice.

Even better.

An entitled surfer.

Done with all the absurd holier-than-thou in the world, irritation flashing hot, she shoved off the chair. Ripped the big sunglasses off her face.

She stomped through perfect groomed sand toward him —kicking the fine grains up, pelting his shins with the stuff —and invaded his personal space.

Hadn't planned the sand-assault.

But incidental weapons worked.

There. How does that feel?

She glared up at Mr. Arrogant, crowding all up in his grill, chest heaving with furious indignation. Unafraid. Preparing to unleash a torrent of pent-up frustration on an easy target.

But the moment her lips parted, her breath caught.

Dark long-lashed eyes stared down at her, sparkling with mirth. From a pretty-boy handsome face. Thick black brows. Dark brown-sugar skin. Defined cheekbones.

Sexy days-old scruff. Which on him, instead of shouting slob, lent a subtler air of indifference. And did nothing to hide a strong angular jawline. Or his full tawny lips. Which twitched once at the corners. As if he fought a smile threatening to break out.

The base female part of her struggled to ignore his shirtless muscular chest. Muscular in a lean athletic would-never-bother-to-lift-weights way.

"What?" All she managed. One measly monosyllable.

She stared him straight in the eyes.

Eyes that crinkled a bit at their outer edges.

His head tilted the slightest fraction. "What do you mean, 'what'?"

"What's so funny?"

She backed up a step and crossed her arms.

Needing to establish a safe zone. Some kind of protection.

Maybe she *did* need blocking. From the bewildering effects of Mr. Arrogant.

Because, somehow, all the harsh words lined up in her brain had fallen away. And her wound-up fury had begun to dissipate.

The guy had a powerful natural presence. To a mind-blowing level.

She blew out a measured exhale, attempting to right herself on shifted ground.

The misshapen top of his head tilted a fraction more. As if he sized her up. Analyzed what, exactly, amused him.

"Your misplaced anger." Spoken with calm indifference. Cool. Confident.

And wow. *So on the nose.*

She blinked heavily, uncertain how to reply. Thrown by the situation.

Mr. Arrogant had pegged her. Without even knowing her.

A first.

Even among guys she'd dated for months.

And people she'd been around all her life.

She glanced farther up, then scowled. At the other thing about the guy that she'd been blinded to. What she'd apparently ignored harder than the rest of him. A jovial red Santa hat. Big white pom at the bottom, resting on a brown squared shoulder. Fluffy white fringe at the top, tugged high, past a black hairline.

The thing sat askew on his head, like an afterthought. As if Mr. Arrogant wore the festive accessory in spite of his coolness. Or maybe because of his obvious self-assuredness.

She had fled from all things Christmas. Yet in a striking coincidence, in the harsh light of early morning, on a first attempt of relaxation at the edge of civilization, there it was. The universe had chased her down and thrown yuletide in her face.

While throwing the sexy Mr. Arrogant her way for good measure.

Talk about off-balance. She didn't know if she should be pissed off… or intrigued.

"Nice hat." Great. Two syllables that time. Making progress. Basic speech. All she seemed capable of around him.

That slight twitch happened at the corners of his mouth again. Almost imperceptible.

He turned his head, glanced off toward her right. Then leveled a hard stare back at her.

"Ready?"

She furrowed her brow. Then glanced off where he had. Beyond a tree with a giant canopy. Toward an elevated peninsula of sunny grass-covered land.

"*Forrr*…" Him to leave? And take his shade-throwing surfboard with him?

He hiked a thumb toward the surfboard—which turned out to be a resort activities board—beside a marked message at the top of it: YOGA 8AM.

"Class."

He arrowed a deadpan at her.

Then he walked away. Leaving the surfboard planted where it stood, deep in the sand.

TWO

KOA STRODE ACROSS THE SAND. Didn't bother turning back around. Didn't need to.

He had hooked Little Miss Attitude. Using a heavy dose of her own medicine.

Her type blew through the island often. Full of themselves. Spent on life. Needing to escape their reality so bad, they vibrated with the desperation of it.

Hair-trigger on the emotions too.

Yet what most wayward vacationers failed to realize? *Can't escape what you bring with you.*

This one struck him as different, though.

Had from the moment she'd caught him off guard.

But not right at that moment, not there on the beach.

From the night before. After he'd pulled a late bar shift. When he'd spotted her standing on the polished travertine in the resort's lobby. She'd distanced herself as far back as possible from a family of seven others checking in. Mom and dad. Twin sisters, about high school age. Auntie and uncle. And a much older auntie, grandmother, maybe.

Or so he'd figured. Based on how alike they all looked.

But it hadn't been just the physical distance from her family that had caught his attention. It had been the forlorn expression. The shallowed breaths. A sparkling in her eyes, from a sheen of tears. Followed by a slight headshake, squared shoulders, and a hard swallow. Then her slow laboring inhale.

Yep. Trouble brewed with that one. *Big* trouble. The down-deep kind that simmered, then pressure-cooked. Threatening to explode.

He knew the warning signs well enough. Had teetered there himself. Not long ago.

Little Miss Attitude stood on the precipice of some monumental shift in her life.

And the trip to paradise?

Was about to shove her off the edge.

Parachute or not.

Last night, he'd thought their paths crossing had been a simple interesting coincidence.

Because he'd been feeling an immense gratitude to be on the final leg of his journey. Right at the exact moment he happened across a lost soul about to embark on hers. He rarely walked through the ostentatious lobby. Had only taken the last-minute detour to get a dose of Hawaiian Christmas. Before he had to leave.

So imagine his surprise when he stumbled across her again the following morning. On his regularly scheduled Thursday morning route. In the least desirable beach area of the sprawling resort.

Not coincidence. Not even close.

More like the greater universe in action. Hurtling two gravitational bodies toward one another. Into a collision course.

Could be a spectacular explosion.

Worth setting fire to that short fuse of hers. See if they'd survive the boom.

Or, at least, explore the possibilities. For the handful of hours he had remaining.

"Hey!" An indignant female shout. From not far behind.

Yep. He'd caught her, for sure. Hook, line, and sinker.

"Yeah?" He didn't turn. Didn't break stride over the sand. Stepped onto the concrete sidewalk. Rounded the red hibiscus hedge. Angled up the path's incline. Veered onto the grass.

"I don't need you to 'school' me."

"Wasn't offering." Wasn't a fool.

A loud sigh huffed out, just behind and beside him. "Oh, but I 'need' yoga?"

"Do you?" She *so* did.

With quick steps, she rushed past him. Slouchy canvas beach bag with rope straps swinging from a shoulder. Red sandals dangling from two fingers. Several paces ahead, she stomped to a halt on the turf, spun to face him, then planted tight fists on her hips. Shapely hips.

"You all but *shouted* it at me."

He paused midstride, soaking in the *haole's* refreshing beauty. Yeah, that had been the other thing that snagged his attention last night. And moments ago, on the beach. That such ugly turmoil could fester under such a pretty exterior.

Not a beauty in the conventional way. Not all painted with make-up. No bleached blondness. No rail-skinny body.

More like striking, in an extraordinary sense. In the deep intensity behind those sparking hazel eyes. With the way she flared the small nostrils of a pert pale nose dusted with freckles. By the nonchalant style of her dark brown hair, scraped into a high messy ponytail, spiky escaped pieces curving every random way.

Fully unaware of her beauty. Natural. Unassuming. Unpretentious.

Stunning.

And for such a diminutive five-foot-nothing, she packed one hell of an attitude. Furious at the world. And anyone who happened to be standing in the way.

"Shouted?" He kept his voice cool and low. Arched a questioning brow at her. "With one word?"

"With that... that... *look*." She narrowed her eyes.

"Interesting." He gave a short nod, then strode on past her.

"What?" She charged ahead again, but then slowed, keeping pace with his easy strides. "*What's* so interesting."

"I didn't know a 'look' could shout."

"Well, yours did," she huffed.

"And how did that make you feel?" Yep. Yoga instructor and therapist.

"*Irritated,*" she grumbled.

Good. At least she had decent self-awareness.

"Up to you, if you want to stay or go. But we'll have to suspend this fascinating discussion. Class is about to start."

Other guests wandered up the grassy incline. Both from the direction of the resort, arriving seconds behind them, and up from the opposite path, curving in from the parking lot.

Timed to the second, actually.

Resulting in Little Miss Attitude's misplaced fury getting cut off.

Not by him, but by the world at large. By the *ten... eleven... thirteen* students who'd showed up. A mix of resort guests and locals, regulars who routinely attended his various classes.

"*Stay*," she announced, dropping the beach bag and red sandals. She then snatched a yellow rolled-up mat from the pile the beach activities crew had made. "I'm staying."

"Good." He shot her a weak smile.

In pleasure or sarcasm.

Little Miss Attitude could take her pick.

Both. As far as he was concerned.

"Because you *do* need it."

THREE

BREATHS SHALLOWING into rapid little gasps of salty air, Brooke fumed.

At Mr. Arrogant.

At herself.

At the whole world.

Mostly, that she'd gotten dragged into the stupid family vacation in the first place.

Right at the worst time in her life.

After she'd spiraled down into the depths of a personal crisis. Unable to endure the deception. Faced with the gravest choice...

Continue on with the lie, become the falsehood... live someone else's life?

Or denounce the forced plan, oust her dutiful-daughter self, and embrace her heart's desire.

Bubbly people in yoga attire bounced past her, snagging spots up front. Wanting to be as close as possible.

To infuriating Mr. Arrogant in his annoying Santa hat?

No thanks.

She stayed put. In the back. Far away from his scrutiny. And his spot-on assessment.

Gusting out a lungful of air, she snapped out her yellow yoga mat, let it fall to the ground, then planted her butt on it. Its sunshiny yellow beamed back at her. Way too cheerful.

Low conversations erupted among small groups of the dozen or so students.

Chest tight and anxiety rising, she ignored them all.

Small talk didn't interest her.

Instead, she gazed out to her right, toward the mass of lava rock jutting out from the ocean. Turbulent waves crashed against the formation. Bright white foam shattered over its stubborn black surface, dancing across it before fading away.

Better. Suited her mood. Stormy.

Her gaze drifted farther out, vision fuzzing as she stared at a deep blue horizon line.

She could still face her parents over the holiday, stand up for herself, for her dreams. Some expensive trip "all about family" didn't have to stop her.

Guilt trips held no sway over her. Hopefully.

And... she didn't need their financial support. Maybe.

A cramp choked the base of her throat over the serious dilemma. Financial support meant more than superfluous things. Money provided food in her mouth, clothes on her back, a roof over her head.

But at what cost?

Not one part of creative her wanted to enter the cold, dry business sector. That was her father's domain.

What she loved more than anything else?

Baking.

Which both of her parents had ridiculed as a whim,

Focus. Clear your mind. What he'd said in the breath exercises. *Surrender your body.* What he'd said next, before bending over, then planting flat palms on his mat.

She was floored at his flexibility. Barely brushed the tips of her fingers on her own mat.

Over the course of the session, she discovered she enjoyed the gentle burn, learning to lean with strength into each pose. And ten or so poses in, she exhaled in grateful relief, rewarded as the tension knots in her muscles began to melt away.

"Well done, class. You're doing great. Now we'll ease into *adho mukha svanasana*, which is Sanskrit for down-ward-facing dog."

Arms outstretched, face down, bent at the waist, she angled her head sideways, straining to see the angle of his body. So she could attempt some semblance of good form.

His Santa hat hung down, white pom touching the mat. Which had somehow over the course of the session become adorable. An integral part of the smartass guy who'd blocked her sun, but had transformed into a sweet, caring knowledgeable yoga instructor. Who appeared to be bent at a perfect ninety-degree angle, heels flat on his mat.

She followed the line of his body. Did her best to bend her hips at the same ideal angle. But her hamstrings, calves, and Achilles had other ideas. She settled for a gentler arch, back at a slight curve, heels a good three inches above her mat.

"And now for our final pose. *Shavasana*, Sanskrit for corpse pose."

She watched him transition into the pose.

Yes. That's *my pose.*

Transitioning from her sad downward dog, she lowered to her knees. Rotated and planted her butt back on the mat.

Then collapsed down into corpse pose. Flat on her back. Arms and legs outstretched. Every muscle relaxed. Mind empty of thought.

Luxurious seconds stretched on. While she melted into the earth.

Muted distant waves crashed. Golden sunrays warmed her muscles. Cool breezes kissed over her skin.

Breaths deepened.

Pulse slowed.

Comforting darkness pulled her down, absorbing her, intertwining her with the island.

"Ready?" Gentle. Bass toned.

She slow-blinked her eyes open. Drew in a deep breath. Pushed herself up, into a seated position on the mat.

The other students had vanished. Only a wide swath of manicured grass remained, colorful mats rolled and stacked into a pile once again.

Koa stood at the end of her yellow mat, hand extended.

"*Forrr...*" Mellow like Jell-O, she didn't bother arguing. Or resisting.

She simply took his offered hand.

Ready? Yep. For anything. Thanks to him.

His warm large hand enveloped hers, then he tugged her up.

"For the rest of our day," he answered. Tone matter-of-fact.

Our. So strange that they'd become an "our" in his mind so fast. And yet, after that soul-altering session? Maybe not so strange at all.

Once she gained her balance, she gave his hand a quick squeeze, then released it.

"I'm Brooke, by the way." They hadn't even introduced

themselves. Yet things felt warm between them. Almost intimate.

"Brooke." He arched a dark brow at her. Amusement sparkled again in those dark eyes. "As in... a stream?"

"Koa." She took a healthy step back, crossing her arms over her chest.

Then she swept a gaze down his still shirtless body. Those sculpted abs. Such trim hips. Over red board shorts with some black tribal design flowing down one side. But she conducted the examination with narrowed eyes, as if sizing up a worthy opponent.

"As in... *wood*?" Yep. Tit for tat.

That fascinating corner-of-the-mouth twitch returned.

He tipped his Santa hat forward, an acknowledging nod.

Annnd... they were back.

"Does 'the rest of our day' include you wearing that ridiculous hat?"

He arched those thick brows. "Does it bother you?"

"Yes."

Not as much as before. But some. On principle, if nothing else.

Those full lips finally broke into a wide smile. "Then, yes."

His eyes searched hers for a moment, as if attempting to puzzle out the mysteries buried somewhere in their depths.

Then he spun around. And strode across the grass. Stepped onto the cement path.

He hooked a right, disappearing behind a yellow hibiscus hedge. Going a different direction than where they'd come from. Away from the resort.

Perfect.

She shouldered her beach bag and toed into her sandals.

Excited.

For the first time in months. Maybe years.

"Wait for me!" she called out.

But she had a hunch, he already was.

And maybe had been. Without knowing it.

Just like her.

FOUR

KOA FOUGHT A SMILE. The day couldn't have been more perfect for a midmorning drive. Blue cloudless sky. Forecasted sixty-nine-degree high. Steady trades.

And a feisty beautiful woman to unravel.

The first ever to capture Koa's serious interest. The only one he'd ever understood, at a glance. Bone deep. Someone much like him. And who might understand him in return.

They only had one day to find out, which sucked. But that was all the universe had in store.

He hoped to make every minute count.

Brooke strode beside him—red sandals soft-slapping her heels with each step—but continued to drop slightly behind. To keep an eye on him? To slow him down? Unspoken doubt?

Regardless, he slowed his pace every time. Wanting to be with her. To ease any uncertainty she might have. Might not even be aware of.

The curving path spilled into the Black Plumeria's overflow parking lot. One his regulars used for its convenient proximity to the yoga lawn. And local beachgoers used for easy access. Smooth black asphalt, fresh white stripes, and a variety of majestic blooming trees made it as well-maintained as the rest of the resort grounds.

But at nine in the morning, after his yoga students had split, only a dozen or so vehicles remained.

His four-door Jeep Wrangler sat, backed in, in a second-row space. He gave his students the closer spots, out of respect.

"This is it." He strode ahead, then offered her a hand. To assist her up into the passenger seat.

She stopped a dozen steps short. Crossed her arms. Expression screwed into intense doubt. "This is... *what?*"

"My Jeep. Our ride."

She arched her brows. Lowered those big round sunglasses. As if an unfiltered stare might change the ride situation. "*Where's* the rest of it?"

"This is all of it." All the parts that mattered. Solid dark-gray frame. Welded roll bars. Newer stocky tires. So what if it didn't have the doors on? Or the roof. Made for a gorgeous open-air drive.

She frowned. "Is it safe?"

"As long as I don't drive us off a cliff."

After two shallow breaths, she drew in a deeper one. She shook her head, but then finally closed the distance between them.

"Here we go," she grumbled, taking his hand.

He guided her safely inside. Then rounded the front and got in beside her.

He twisted, leaning back, and retrieved two chilled bottles of water. From the small cooler wedged into the floorboard behind her seat.

After he handed her one, she guzzled a good third of it down.

He knocked back as much himself, quenching his thirst with the mineralized water.

"*Where* are we going, by the way?" She fastened her seatbelt with a click.

"Does it matter?" With a press of the ignition, the engine rumbled to life.

"Yes." She glared at the Santa hat. Then dropped her gaze to his. Expression dead serious. "*Nowhere* touristy. *Nothing* Christmassy."

"Off the beaten path." *All I had in mind*, he thought, as he drove them out of the lot.

"Exactly. Any cool local places? Somewhere different?"

He snorted. "Only about a thousand of 'em."

"Gee. Sounds special." She dropped her beach bag from her lap to the floorboard between her feet. "Can you narrow that down?"

"We better. All we've got is today." He tried to sound nonchalant about that fact. Bummer that it was. "How 'bout I give you your top three?"

"*My* top three? How will you know?"

He shrugged, turning right, onto the highway. "We'll figure it out as we go."

She seemed to relax at that. Leaned that high messy ponytail back against the headrest.

"I'm going for life-altering here." Had to keep her on her toes.

"Wow." She glanced at him. "Quite a high bar."

He kept his attention on the road ahead. "Quite a demanding woman."

She stared at him a moment longer, through those big dark sunglasses, then shifted her gaze *mauka*, toward the flat barren lava-dotted landscape stretching inland. After a moment, she glanced *makai*, toward the turquoise ocean.

They cruised along at a smooth fifty-five, up and down the highway's dips and hills, curving through slow rises and gentle falls.

The sun warmed them through the open top. While road wind—which played with her loose hair spikes and puffed the sleeves of her black cotton top—cooled them.

She continued to pan her gaze, *mauka* and *makai*, not wanting to miss a thing.

"Goats!" She sat up straighter, pointing to a horned herd of fifteen. Then she scanned the ground on both sides of the road. "Looks like a bleak moonscape."

"From the lava flows. And we're leeward. The arid dry side of the island."

"Are we heading toward something lusher?"

"We are." He wanted to see her take on a different kind of Hawaii. "Do you like coffee?"

She huffed out a snort. "Do you need oxygen?"

Right. "Done. Experience number one? On the way."

"Hmmm..." She knocked back several swallows of water. "Three life-altering experiences. I feel a little like Scrooge."

He shot her a deadpan. "Imagine that."

FIVE

BROOKE VIBRATED with a wild kind of energy. It rushed through her like nothing she'd ever felt before.

Dangerous. Exciting.

A bit like fear.

But budding with hope.

Hope that maybe the deadened part of her, deep within her broken heart, had stirred back to life.

Through the nearly hour of open highway driving, they'd exchanged small talk. He'd spouted island factoids, like the names of the five volcanoes and stats on their levels of activity. She'd asked about features she spotted, like the striking peekaboo sections of turquoise ocean: Kua Bay and Makalawena Beach.

Then, not far into their easygoing driving conversation, both of their forearms resting on the Jeep's padded center console, his fingers had brushed hers.

She'd gasped at the unexpected contact, pulse jumping. But as that delightful thrill still tripped through her, she brushed his fingers back.

They'd entwined their fingers together for the rest of

the drive. Sometimes stretching, then flexing. Sometimes rubbing, like his thumb on the back of her hand. But always connected.

And to her shock, after only knowing the guy a couple of hours, she liked it.

Then again, in some strange and wonderful way, it felt like she'd known him forever.

On the final quarter of their drive, they'd turned inland —*mauka*, he'd explained—climbing up into a part of the island that was cast straight from her romantic imaginings.

Dense jungle crowded in on a narrow winding two-lane road.

Clusters of old shops and quaint galleries speckled here and there, along slim gravel shoulders. Some weathered buildings hid in the deep shadows of giant trees. A lucky few got bathed in the golden glow of late-morning sunlight.

On the last mile, they'd encountered a series of sandwich-board signs, each several hundred feet from the last, warning of coffee ahead. So that any parched jittery soul in dire need of a hit of caffeine—like her—wouldn't miss it.

And then, seconds ago, Koa had parked in the property's narrow upper lot.

After they climbed out, she shouldered her beach bag.

He reached into a duffel stowed behind his seat and pulled out an olive short-sleeved tee. On the back of the shirt, curled a cool black shark, a vivid colorful Hawaiian scene inside the shark's body.

He plucked the Santa hat off, in order to shrug into the tee.

Then, with a smug look toward her, he tugged the Santa hat back on. And the thing hung precariously on his head, even more askew than before.

"Didn't want to disappoint you." He waggled his brows.

She stepped close, tugging the hat down a little. Which tucked several thick black curls under its fluffy white fringe.

He entwined his fingers into her free hand, then pulled her against him.

She collided against his body with a gasp of surprise.

Before she had a chance to react further, he dipped his head down. And brushed those full tawny lips over hers. Warmth flowed through her, from the sensual point of their first kiss, straight to her heart.

She melted against him, lips softening, breath hitching.

He deepened the kiss, then groaned.

After long delicious seconds, he eased backward.

He rested his forehead against the top of hers. While they sucked in heavy deep breaths.

The world seemed to shift even further.

"Been wanting to do that for a while," he murmured.

"I'm glad you did."

Hand in hand, her heart soaring, they climbed down a wide lava-stone staircase.

They passed a sundries shop, strolled across a lawn trimmed by beds of culinary herbs, then wandered into the shade of a covered lanai.

Drawn by the incredible view, she wandered toward a high long counter that stretched along an organic wooden railing. The spot overlooked hundreds of rows of trellises.

"That's coffee?" With its sprawling hillside of terraces, the property resembled a vineyard.

"Yep." He draped an arm around her shoulder. "First ever trellised coffee. Kona Joe has won tons of awards."

"Wow." The vision stole her breath away. Tall skinny papaya trees and massive shade-throwing Koa trees dotted through the terraced coffee plants. Down beyond, stretched a vast deep-blue ocean, beneath the gentler blue of a cloudless sky.

She leaned against him, basking in his protective warmth. Inhaling the earthy, salty natural scent of him.

The place was beautiful, serene.

And in Koa's arms, a man who seemed to get her from their first meeting? Beyond romantic.

A sudden sound of loud grinding pierced through her reverie, popping her head up.

"*Coffee*." Like a woman possessed, she pushed out of his arms and rushed to the far wall where a coffee bar stretched before a line of three customers.

Only a hint of Christmas decorated the bar. Small red bows pinning up green garland.

The man ahead of her engaged the female barista in brief conversation.

Brooke caught the tail end of the gentleman's convo after perusing the overhead menu board, right as Koa stepped beside her. He entwined their fingers together again. Gave her a gentle hip bump.

She returned the hip bump. Incredulous that only two short hours ago she'd stumbled onto a beach chair. Seconds before Koa had blocked her sun.

The barista beckoned her forward.

"Quad-shot Americano, please." Plenty of caffeine. With some amount of hydration.

"Same," Koa said.

"Did I overhear you say you just moved here?" she asked the barista.

"Yep." The young woman gave a nod.

"From where? If you don't mind me asking."

"Not at all." The energetic woman flitted about behind the bar, filling drink orders. "I'd been traveling around.

Nomad style. Couchsurfing. A few budget hotels. All across America, South America, Australia, Asia. Then I came here. And never left."

Wow. That said something. After having globetrotted a vast distance. "How long ago?"

"Nine months."

"And what's the verdict?" Brooke hungered for every morsel of a newcomer's view. "Do you regret staying?"

The barista gave her a headshake and a wide smile. "Not even a little."

"Did you know anyone else here?"

"Back then?" She slid their two Americanos across the bar. "Nope. Not a one."

"Thanks." Brooke gave her a nod.

"Aloha," the barista said in parting.

She sat with Koa at one of the bistro tables. While they sipped decadent coffee. Staring at the best view in the world.

In the background, on a large monitor above the bar, the story of Kona Joe streamed. An incredible romantic story about how he vacationed to the island, met and fell in love with his beautiful Hawaiian wife, and never left.

Two inspiring stories of brave adventure.

One that happened decades ago. The other mere months.

She wondered how many others had taken that leap of faith, never looking back.

Because the idea of coming to an island and never leaving?

Terrifying.

And absolutely thrilling.

SIX

WITH EVERY HOUR that passed on their three-experi-
ence tour, as the clock counted down the few hours Koa had
remaining, Brooke burrowed deeper into his heart.

For a person on the brink of a life-changing moment,
she handled the pressure well.

He envied her.

With her unexpected arrival, the solid ground beneath
his feet had begun to shift again.

And he had no idea how to survive his coming
departure.

Whether the two of them had any hope for time after he
left...

Or if one perfect day in paradise was all they got.

No matter which it turned out to be, he'd cherish their
incredible moments together.

They climbed the curvy road that led *mauka*, into
upcountry. Where the second and third experiences waited.

"You've gone really quiet." She glanced at him. Those
big round sunglasses shielding her hazel eyes from him.
Wisps of dark hair whipping across her forehead.

"Sorry. Lost in thought."

"About?" She clutched her black Kona Joe cup with both hands, taking a sip through its dark plastic lid.

"Us." There. He'd spit the emo-topic out.

"There's an 'us'?"

Surprise vibrated through her lifted tone. Or had that been hope?

He shrugged, uncertain where she stood. "Dunno." Casual. In case the heavy feeling was only from his side. "Is there?"

Silence dragged for long seconds.

When he glanced over, she stared out through the windshield. Gaze unfocused. As if lost in her own thoughts.

She sucked in a slow breath. "What did you mean when you said 'All we've got is today'?"

"I'm leaving tonight." Horrific timing.

"When, tonight?" Disappointment deadened her tone.

He understood the feeling. "Midnight flight."

"To where?"

"Bali. To visit my family."

"You're family lives in Bali?"

"Yep. Dad manages a five-star resort there. I grew up in 'em. Handful of years at any given place. Traveling all over the world."

"You're not Hawaiian?"

"Part Hawaiian. Mom's half-Hawaiian half-Japanese. Dad's half-Hawaiian half-Indian."

More silence. She took another sip from her tightly clutched coffee.

"What about you?" he asked, trying to diffuse the tension.

"I'm a melting pot. German. English. Irish. Italian. A little Russian."

"And your parents?" He blurted the words without thinking them through. Sliding right out onto thin ice. Remembering her trauma in the lobby, her literal distancing from them.

At her extended silence, he attempted some sort of recovery. "What do they do?"

She sighed, expression clouding. "Business." Tone deadened.

"Ah." He matched her deadened tone. U-turning them out of that dead-end.

He grabbed his coffee out of the holder. Glugged down several large swallows. Then seated it back down.

"What brought you here?" she ventured, tone brightening a little. "To Big Island. Did your dad manage a resort here?"

"No. I came here alone. On my own. To make something of myself."

She glanced toward him, brows raising over the sunglass rims. "And have you?"

"Almost. You'll see part of the dream in just a second." They crossed a bridge at a curve in the road. The landscape grew lusher with every passing block.

They began to enter the rural outskirts of Waimea. Rolling hills shifting from short dry grasses to verdant pastureland, dotted with black grazing cattle.

He turned off the highway, heading down a narrow curving drive. Through a corridor of purple-blooming jacaranda trees. To a sprawling estate. Rundown. But still standing.

When he stopped and cut the engine, they both got out, then began to wander toward the dilapidated property. Apart, but angling toward one another as they drew closer to the front steps.

Their hands met as they reached the edge of the manor, where overgrown grasses met dry-rotted wood.

"What's this place?" She lifted her sunglasses, parking them atop her head.

"A possibility."

"*Forrr...*"

He shrugged. "Bed and breakfast? A place to host guests. Teach yoga. Tend bar."

She blinked up at him. "You're a bartender too?"

"And a house framer. Sometimes painter. Most islanders have several jobs. Helps drag us out of poverty."

"And you're aiming to run your own place someday."

"Yep." Be his own boss, with a cool place of his own. "Someday soon."

"You've saved that much already? After how long?"

"Six-and-a-half years." Ever since he turned eighteen.

Hand in hand, they stared at the old place for a while in silence.

Then they wandered around the property. Poking around the perimeter of the house. Peering through dirty, but intact, windows. Picking their way through overgrown gardens, under vine-covered pergolas.

When they circled back toward the front, she kept hold of his hand, and they climbed the rotted front steps with care, then turned around.

They gazed at the most spectacular view on Big Island. Down the sloping pasturelands. To the vast Pacific stretching far and wide.

She drew in a slow deep breath. "Does that possibility, might it have... an 'us'?"

He squeezed her hand, then pulled her close. Staring down into her beautiful hazel eyes, his throat constricted. He swallowed hard past the lump, then arched his brows.

"A guy can only hope."

SEVEN

BROOKE'S HEAD spun as they drove back under the arching purple jacarandas, leaving the rundown property. The place of Koa's dreams. Or someplace like it.

A possibility.

And the idea of leaping into an ocean of possibilities, appealed to her.

Especially the one possibility sitting right beside her.

Which scared the hell out of her.

But... more than that, it brightened her newfound hope a little more.

The short drive from that property to their third and final experience sobered her a bit.

They traveled in comfortable silence. While she swiveled her head back and forth, taking in the rural beauty of Waimea. Architecture that varied from cozy post-pier bungalows to grand mansions. Store fronts and small shopping plazas that evoked a ranching vibe, structures with painted siding in bright cheery colors.

A wonderful cooling mist flowed through Waimea,

funneled up by the trades through Waipi'o Valley on the island's windward side, Koa had explained.

Christmas abounded through the vibrant small upcountry town. Including a giant island pine in its center, strung with colored lights. Fences featured lit white snowflakes. Lampposts were spiraled with red bows. Parking lot signs were draped with red-and-green garlands.

Even the circular drive Koa turned down had been decked in painted candy canes.

He parked beside a small steepled building. When they got out, he clasped her hand, then led her toward another similar building. Part of a church?

"First Christmas Eve experience, into the past..." The story of travelers, arriving on Big Island, and never leaving.

He gave her a nod, pausing at a bend in the sidewalk. "Then we hit the present. My favorite dilapidated estate. Filled with potential."

"Lots of possibilities." About his dream. And the idea of that "us."

"Now, an investment in a future." For the first time all day, he reached up and adjusted the Santa hat. As if now, how he looked, or that the hat sat on his head, mattered to him.

After a last glance down at her, then a deep breath, he turned and tugged her forward.

He led her toward a giant white tent.

Where a dozen people all wore aprons. Stood in front of silver chafing dishes. Spooned out food onto plates. Handed them back over to various folks, a long line of waiting diners.

"A food kitchen?"

He gave her a nod. "Community meal. In-person and delivered. Feeds hundreds every week."

The joy in the volunteers faces brought warmth to her heart.

Even better? The warm smiles and friendliness of all the diners. Kids and adults. Singles, couples, and families. All ages. A melting pot of nationalities.

"Want to help?" He arched his brows.

"Yes. Absolutely."

And in her heart of hearts, she knew she'd stumbled across something incredible.

With Koa and the world of possibilities he'd shown her.

The decision she faced, no longer a simple matter of businesswoman versus baker.

What amazing things could she do if she transplanted into a world like Koa's? Where dreams became reality. Anything she dared to imagine. Worked hard toward. Earned. With true passion. While giving to others, with deep compassion.

After a heartwarming hour of serving Christmas Eve dinners at the community meal, they tugged their aprons over their heads, got back into his Jeep, then headed back down the mountain.

Down toward the resort.

Back toward her demanding family.

Annnd... toward the end of her day with Koa.

"Sooo... Midnight. Tonight." The stroke of midnight on their fairy tale clock. When the princess turned back into the maid. The Jeep into a pumpkin.

Fate had relegated them to be star-crossed lovers.

"Yeah. After a few hours tending bar."

Her hopes lifted. Eager to take whatever she could get. "At the resort?"

"Yeah." He glanced at her. "But the bar will be packed. We won't have any time together."

Oh. "Maybe at the end?"

"Yeah. Maybe." That rich bass tone sounded crestfallen.

Which burned a gloomy hole deep into her chest.

But then, hope blossomed anew. "When do you get back?"

"Three weeks. Second week of January."

"Ah." Dammit. "The week after I leave."

If she left.

EIGHT

TENDING bar at the resort had never been so excruciating. Four hours long. Till eleven. Then a mad dash to the airport. Twenty minutes away.

Before Koa's shift, he and Brooke shared one more blessed hour at the resort.

Where they made out like rabid teens. Hiding behind bushes. And every other secret spot. Each time, cover blown by random guests, also seeking private romance.

But never her parents. Or any member of her family.

He'd felt a bit like Johnny in *Dirty Dancing*. Sneaking around with Baby.

And yet, he'd do it all over again. Keep things under wraps. For those last precious stolen moments.

After a final heated kiss, where they'd sat together on the lounge chair he'd met her on—her with those big sunglasses perched on her head, him with the Santa hat she'd grown to love—he walked away. All by mutual agreement. No tearful goodbyes. No sappy words.

Off program, he'd had to suffer through watching her

enter the restaurant. She'd come in with her entire family. Then glanced his way, mouthing *I'm sorry*.

Not her fault. The bar sat in the middle of Black Plumeria's best restaurant. And fine dining on Christmas Eve came at a premium. Booked months in advance.

If her family had done so, she'd gotten dragged into the torture right along with him.

She'd also chosen not to share whatever personal dilemma she faced. Continued to stand on that personal precipice alone.

He didn't blame her. Had been there himself.

A person got ready to share when they could handle it. However long the process took. And not a moment sooner.

Besides, it kept their last moments untarnished. As much as possible. Given the difficult circumstances.

Nothing like finding love. At the worst possible time.

Halfway through his shift, around 9pm, the tension at her table escalated. Furious expressions from her parents. Shouted words, even though he couldn't hear them over the live island Christmas music.

Her father shot up, chair wobbling back, nearly toppling. He tossed his napkin down and stormed off. Her mother chased after him. Both had worn such deep frowns, their faces looked ready to crack.

The twin younger sisters seemed delighted by all the drama.

Auntie and uncle? Stunned.

The grandmother, with a snowy white bun spun atop her head, got up from her place across the table. Then she sat next to Brooke, wrapping her arms around her granddaughter.

From the moment of the reveal, whatever it had been,

Brooke slumped. With heavy guilt, if he ever saw it. And disappointment.

Brooke inhaled a shaky breath. As her grandmother consoled her.

All while Koa could do nothing. By their agreement. Per his job. And because Brooke needed to take her leap off that cliff alone. Because she hadn't asked for his help, hadn't shared her problem with him.

But more than all that, she had to make that stand for herself *by herself*. Only way to make it stick.

When she left, an hour before he had to bolt, she didn't glance up at him.

Lost in her old sorrows, he figured. Still in shock over the reaction. In a mental loop over the heated exchange. Maybe even mourning a loss.

And then he stood there behind the bar. Alone. Yet busy as hell on Christmas Eve, thank God. Which made the shift fly by.

Then at eleven, he left the bar. Grateful for the time he and Brook had shared. Thoughts spinning back and sticking to only the best parts of the day.

Mind numb, he retrieved his bag from his work locker, then drove straight to the airport.

While staring at the dark ribbon of road, he focused on his breaths.

Deep inhale for a count of four…

Hold for a count of four…

Exhale for a slow count of eight…

He'd already printed his boarding pass early that morning. Before they'd met.

The small outdoor airport, under the darkness of a crisp clear night, seemed a ghost town.

Five passengers besides him sat in the waiting area. All looking as bleary-eyed as him.

The overhead announcement called out his flight number to Bali.

He stood, then trudged forward, feet cement blocks.

The ball of his Santa hat shifted off his shoulder, as he handed the uniformed ticket agent his boarding pass.

Then he stepped through the gate. Walked across the tarmac. Started the climb of the outer ramp, up the switchbacks, behind other passengers destined for the lengthy flight to Bali.

Something hard collided into his back, stumbling him forward up the ramp.

Adrenaline spiking, he spun around, tangled up in whatever had nailed him.

Brooke.

She stood against him, and half around him. Arms breaking away for a brief second as he turned. Before she rushed forward again, clamping him in a huge bear hug.

"Brooke?" He frowned, confused.

Shocked that she stood there.

Overjoyed. Stunned. And overwhelmed.

"Room for one more on your trip?" Unshed tears glistened in her eyes.

A Santa hat, just like his, clung to her head.

Behind her? She'd parked a large green wheeled suitcase.

"Isn't that a bit much? Meeting my parents after only one day?"

Her breath caught. Her lower lip wobbled, then she tugged it in with her teeth.

"*Heyyy...*" He tugged her into his arms. "I just *meant,* sure you can handle that kind of pressure?"

She coughed out a half-laugh half-cry as tears streamed down her beautiful face.

"Yeah. After what I just went through?" she muttered. "Piece of cake."

"Cool." He gave her a tender kiss. Because he'd missed her. And his heart had broken over the idea of losing her.

She deepened the kiss. Apparently as happy and grateful at their reunion as he was. Maybe more so.

When the flight attendants shouted at them from the open door of the plane, an entire switchback of ramp above them, he broke away.

Then he dropped his forehead to hers. "And I expect a full report. About everything. Every little detail of your life. No holding back." The time for secrets had come and gone.

She snorted. "You sure we have time?"

"You know how long this flight is, don't you?"

Her brow furrowed. She gave a slight headshake. "No."

"Thirteen hours."

Her eyes widened. But then a beautiful smile curved her lips.

"Perfect." Pure happiness brightened her face. "That we get all those minutes. Alone."

"Well..." He thought about the other few passengers. About the long ride to his parents' place on a local bus. About his enormous extended family. Crammed into a not-so-enormous house. "*Almost.*"

EPILOGUE

THE FOLLOWING YEAR, at Christmastime, Brooke had gone all out, had totally decked the halls.

Several of the halls, to be exact. Inside that dilapidated old property. *Their* old property. Made new. Well... almost.

It had been a labor of love. And remained a work in progress.

Because over that thirteen-hour flight to Bali, she'd shared everything with Koa.

Including all the emotional turmoil she'd suffered through the past several years. Her hate for all things business. Her new appreciation for Christmas decorations. And her forever love for baking.

But as it turned out, the only business she hated was big business.

Small bed and breakfasts? Her new passion.

And another brand-new discovery, made on the island? Her incredible love for sourdough. Tangy beautiful sourdough. Which had been the first thing she'd made after they'd revved up one of the two commercial-grade kitchens on the property. And then she'd begun experimenting.

Turned out the old place had two kitchens. Ten bedrooms, in the main house. Two sizable *ohanas* (separate guest houses). Three dining rooms, two medium-sized and one enormous.

Four gardens. Two lawns, one for yoga and one for croquet, according to Koa.

Plenty of room for a decent bed and breakfast.

Over the last ten months, while they worked on renovations, the place had become a home to several of Koa's coworkers, from the resort and his construction jobs. Who all not only paid what they could afford, but also chipped in with labor in exchange for room and board.

The place was just beginning to come together.

All thanks to his dream, their one amazing day, and her incredible leap of faith.

Oh, and thanks to Gran. Their silent partner. Who'd funded Brooke's part of the down payment and co-signed on their loan.

Someday soon, maybe sometime over the next year, they'd have a real bed and breakfast. Up and running.

Koa sidled up next to her, wrapping his arms around her.

She sighed with contentment as he pressed a soft kiss to her temple.

"Ready?" he murmured.

"*Forrr...*" She turned to face him. Her handsome man had grown a decent beard over the last few weeks.

They both wore Santa hats.

"Christmas dinner. Everyone's waiting."

Out beyond their renovated kitchen, which they'd painted off-white, its hardwood floors sanded and stained, with fresh-picked herbs in glass mason jars on a windowsill overlooking the courtyard.

Past a bare sheetrock hallway, down into the only fully finished dining room. Medium-sized. Painted a soft ivory, original wood paneling restored to a rich sheen, and outfitted with a long reclaimed-wood table and mismatched chairs, some carved-wood keepers, some functional for-nows.

A warm and inviting room, decorated to the hilt, with a trimmed Christmas tree (grown right there on Big Island), a dozen potted white poinsettias, and red stockings jam-packed together on the long mantel above a large gray soap-stone fireplace.

And filled with family.

Their new family. One she'd grown closer to. All through the year.

Koa and her. And Gran, who'd flown out to be with them. And all of Koa's friends—her new friends. The family that mattered.

The ones who loved you no matter what.

And who made wild impossible dreams come true.

HALF-BAKED HOLIDAY

ONE

ANNA CREPT through the front door of the historic home, equal parts anxious fear and curious excitement churning in her gut.

At that early-evening hour, twilight glowed through the floral stained glass windows, inset into the entry's double doors and the single transom above them. The effect cast soft blues, greens, and pinks through the square front hall, washing the wooden benches, rose-painted walls, and white crown-molded ceiling into a dreamlike place of the past.

She eased the door closed behind her, holding its embossed round iron knob—and her breath—while the door seated back into its frame, joining its stained glass mate with a low click.

Eyes closing, she paused, waiting. Listening.

But the only sounds were calm. Relaxed. Muted strains of instrumental Christmas music—from one of the upstairs rooms? And low murmurs, from voices in the next room.

No tension. No alarm.

She exhaled a lungful of air and opened her eyes.

So far, so good.

A slower inhale gifted her with the scents of antique wood. Tinged with notes of fresh pine and a hint of cinnamon.

A brisk December cold from outside still pricked at her numb face and hands. The firm decision to go without coat, hat, and snow boots, had even threatened her core body temperature. But within seconds of slipping indoors, the bone-deep chill had begun to fade.

As she'd expected.

Which had made the fifteen minutes of stalking around through a light snow bearable. Traveling along the edge of campus, creeping through bushes and alongside buildings—in a thin turtleneck and wool cable-knit sweater, thick corduroy pants, and nimble hiking boots.

She tiptoed farther inside the old house. Edging along its hardwood flooring in the fervent hope of avoiding tattle-tale creaks. Skirting a loaded coatrack in the front corner. Pressing against a skinny patch of wall, beside a square-cased opening that separated the entrance hall from the front parlor.

Taking another pause, she listened again, verifying she'd gone detected. Then she snuck a daring peek around the corner. She exposed only half an eye past the wide wood casing, a rich fluted rosewood that stretched from floor to ceiling and spanned all the way around the ten-foot opening.

She spied on the last Christmas tour of the year.

And determined they were clearing the front parlor and entering the sitting room. The official group of eight was herded by a familiar low-timbered elderly female docent, who droned on with facts about the beautiful Queen Anne and the original family who'd lived there for generations.

Anna watched the backs of the adult tourists, grouped

in twos and a threesome, while the last stragglers disappeared from view.

She waited another cautious handful of seconds, doing her best to slow her shallowed breaths. Then she crept into the vacated parlor, hugged the short wall she'd just rounded, and began to inch her way around the large bay window. While she squeezed between the three windows' frothy white sheers and a giant Christmas tree that dripped sparkling silver, snowy white, and cherry red trimmings, lit by a billion white lights. And while stepping over the scalloped edges of a red brocade tree skirt, hemmed with slender twists of cherry silk cord and accented by fat cherry tassels.

Being careful not to kick any of the dozens of wrapped faux-presents.

And doing her damnedest not to get tripped up by any of it: clingy draperies, snaggy tree stuff, or hiding electrical cords.

Hoping not to get spotted by some passerby outside, while lit up through the windows.

All of a sudden, her foot snagged.

On... something.

She tried to look down, but glittering ornaments, snowy garland, and tree boughs strung with dozens of lights blocked her view.

Shifting her weight left, she retracted her right foot and lifted, to clear whatever snag had tripped her up.

But in the awkward one-legged position, she lost her balance. Kicked her right leg down. And knocked her left arm into the tree.

A riot of tinkling burst into the silence, delicate ornaments chiming their alarm.

The knocked tree listed forward.

"Oh, *no...*" she whispered, horrified.

No no no no no...

The tree tipped farther into its slow-motion sway.

Without thought, she plunged her arms into its depths—to the repeated tinkling protest of the ornaments—grabbing the rough branches with both hands. Prickliness stabbed and chafed against her clutching fingers, but she didn't care. Couldn't afford to.

And to her utter relief, with that desperate two-handed grasp, the tree stabilized.

Closing her eyes, she gusted out a grateful sigh.

Then inch by slow inch, she pulled, leaning gently back, against the filmy sheer and cold glass.

Fretful long seconds later, the tree settled back into its full upright position.

She released her clenched grip on the branches, but held fast, hovering her opened hands there. When the tree remained motionless, she extracted her arms with great care, trying not to jostle the ornaments.

Then she waited, chewing the corner of her lower lip with worry.

But as more torturous seconds dragged by, no alarmed tourist—or docent—appeared.

Satisfied the racket had sounded louder to her in the bay window bell, but hadn't traveled far enough to alert the others, she pressed both hands back against the filmy sheer to the cold windowpane. And braced by the wiser support of both hands, she lifted her right foot high, clearing whatever trap she'd sprung before, then toed her boot down to land a solid step into a safe landing zone.

She proceeded the rest of the way through the bay window like that, both hands braced, one foot lifted, then toe planted on solid ground. Followed by another balanced, measured step. Three points of stable contact at all times.

Once she made it through the tree-gauntlet without further incident, she let out a sigh.

And refusing to get spooked by the close call, she moved on with her plan.

She inched past a tall footed radiator. Which radiated zero heat. Even though the charming cast iron relic appeared brand-new. With rich black paint under elaborate pale rose filigree that adorned the corners and edges of each of its ten fins.

Once clear of the radiator, she plastered herself against tasteful wallpaper. Which depicted arching stylized sage-green fronds, embellished with highlights of silver, painted on a buttercream backdrop.

Creeping another few feet sideways, she sidled up beside an impressive ornate fireplace. Small rectangular sage tiles surrounded its unused firebox. Which was all framed by a deep columnar mantel and top assembly, carved of rosewood. Two beautiful flat cornices—one high above the inset mirror, one below the mantel shelf—were adorned by delicate carved garlands whose peaks were graced by bows.

She hid in the shadows of one of the fireplace's large fluted side columns. It towered toward the ceiling, topped by a carved-leaf capital that flared into the parlor's matching rosewood crown molding.

Then she waited. Again.

But uneventful seconds ticked by.

All appeared calm after her idiotic tree-tangle.

She exhaled a slow breath. And lowered her tensed shoulders. A fraction.

Stage one. Secure the parlor, unseen. Check.

From her new hiding spot, she spied on the group of nine again. One eye peering through festive camouflage on the mantel: between a fearsome red-and-white nutcracker sentry armed with a candy cane and the fluffy silver-and-white garland strung with white lights at his feet.

She bided her time, staking out the tour. Watching. And listening.

While they examined framed photos and news clippings, memorabilia that had been mounted on the sitting room's walls by the college town's historical society.

From the choice vantage point, she also saw clear through to the sitting room's far central door. Which had been propped open. And led into the home's central hall and red-carpeted stairs.

A cold draft chilled through her turtleneck and sweater, and she shivered.

No warmth from the radiator.

No heat from the fireplace.

And why bother?

After the tour, the place got buttoned up tight for winter break. From tomorrow's Christmas Eve all the way through New Year's Day.

She drew in a slower breath, attempting to calm her still-jangled nerves. And wrinkled her nose at the faint musty odor hovering around her fireplace corner.

A sinus tickle formed.

Then a sneeze threatened.

She clamped a hand over her mouth and nose.

No. No. No no nooo...

Unable to prevent it, she slammed her face into the muffling elbow of her sweater, pinched her eyes shut, and sneezed. Twice.

Great. Why not grab a megaphone and announce your arrival?

But when she glanced up and peered through the mantel's garland, the docent seemed unfazed. She gave a double-clap, then turned, leading a migration out the sitting room's hall door. Seconds later, the herd clomped up the carpeted wooden staircase.

Perfect!

Still undetected.

And right on time.

After the last set of boots disappeared from view, she darted through the sitting room, rushed into the empty hall, then pushed through an adjoining door.

She paused, waiting. Back plastered to the door she'd just closed. Pulse hammering a tense beat against her eardrums.

But no reaction followed her burst of energy. No alarms sounded. No clomping footfalls returned.

She exhaled a sigh of relief once again.

One room at a time. One stage of the plan after another.

Shaking body braced against the solid wood door, the separation between her and the rest of the home's occupants, she worked to slow her breaths again.

And her thumping heart began to calm, somewhat.

All while she drank in the beauty of the forbidden space she'd invaded: the kitchen.

An off-limits part of the house she'd been *jonesing* to explore. For days.

Unauthorized, for the official tour. Per the droning docent.

Stage Two. Take the kitchen, unseen. Check.

Which gave her about six more minutes. Per the plan. And her internal clock.

A low thud resonated. Unusual. Loud.
She froze, holding her breath.
A floorboard creaked.
Both somewhere nearby. *Not* upstairs.
Great. Maybe she had no time at all.
And had seriously miscalculated.
Everything.

TWO

JONATHAN BIT OUT A CURSE. Under his breath. Standing in total darkness. Trapped in a closet.

Or, judging by the battling spices lingering in the air... a pantry.

But he didn't dare move.

Not yet.

He'd gone too deep. Had come so far.

Lured by a beautiful mysterious woman.

Who seemed to be stalking an innocent home tour.

While he stalked her.

He'd been bored out of his mind. Stuck in the small college town he'd grown up in. For another eternal Christmas break. Family obligations, and all that.

But that night, not two blocks off campus, crossing the street to head for O'Malley's Bar, he'd caught the most unusual sight.

The silhouette of a woman in the old Kennifort House. While she crept along the narrow space between that year's giant Christmas tree and the front bay window.

Intrigued enough to investigate closer, he'd veered

toward the house, then ambled up its cobblestone walkway. He stared toward the best corner of the house, which he admired whenever he walked by. Dark sandstone foundation blocks supported that large bay window. And above and beyond it, a square balcony's rising turret was capped by two ornate finials, making a complicated and appealing second-story roofline.

He'd glanced over just in time to catch the woman almost yard-sale the tree. Almost.

Coughing out a shocked laugh, he'd paused on the cobblestones.

Then he'd stood there, hands tucked into his jacket pockets. Enthralled by the enigmatic scene. Watching how the woman saved the tree. While a gentle snow dusted him.

And the next few enchanting moments—her pantomimed comedy of cautious stealth—had reeled him all the way in.

Once she'd crept past the bay window, he'd slipped into the house.

When she'd sidled up beside the fireplace, he'd spied from the front hall.

And after she'd raced from the parlor, through the sitting room, out the central hall, and into the kitchen... he'd strolled in her wake. Nice and calm.

Straight down the center of the parlor.

Making a slow curve through the sitting room, into the hall.

But from there, familiar with the layout, he'd taken a detour.

He'd veered into the dining room. Then slipped through an opposite swinging door.

Which he'd *thought* had led into the kitchen.

What he hadn't planned? The total lights-out beyond.

Or the cramped quarters.

He'd entered some kind of closet.

And had whacked his forehead on something hard. Unforgiving immovable hard.

A shelf?

Who the hell put an *overhanging* shelf in a closet? Or a pantry.

Whatever it was, wherever he stood, the room had a door. And he'd seen grown adults rotate in and out of that dining room door during charity events in years past. So, a clear walk-through situation. Therefore, nothing should have beamed him in the head.

He frowned, stumped by the dead end.

His head began to throb with a pounding headache. He probed the spot with his forefinger. And located a sizable sore knot near his hairline.

Great. Chase a woman? Get a concussion.

And yet... *best* Christmas break ever.

Something was afoot.

And he couldn't wait to crack the mystery.

Or be a part of it.

Done with all the cramped dark-and-gloomy, he unzipped his jacket, plucked his phone from the inside pocket, and lit up the space with its flashlight.

Another swinging door, a few feet ahead to his left, got illuminated in the bright glow.

There you go. How serving staff had rotated through before.

So he hadn't completely lost his mind.

He switched the light off, took two steps forward, then eased the door open. Only a tiny crack.

A loud creak groaned at the small movement.

He froze. And held his breath.

But as seconds dragged on, no reaction came.

He stared at the door crack.

Only an inch-and-a-half wide.

Dim twilight glowed through.

Exhaling a slow breath, he leaned forward and angled an eye to the crack.

But he couldn't see a damn thing. Besides a small slice of the kitchen. Part of a window. Gray counter. Brown cabinetry. Corner of a kitchen island.

Nothing else.

He stepped back, taking his hand off the door. And it creaked back closed.

Great.

Stuck in a closet.

A *sweltering* closet.

Sweat dripped between his shoulder blades as growing heat cooked through him.

The closet air felt cool to his clammy face, but he still wore a knit hat and puffer jacket.

He licked his lips, tasting the salt from his sweat. Then he clicked on his phone-flashlight again, lighting up the rest of the space.

Which revealed a stockpile of bone china. And assorted crystal glassware. And serving pieces. Shelves and shelves of the antique stuff, floor to ceiling, on two sides of the L-shaped closet. Dinner, supper, and dessert plates. Various meat platters and soup tureens. Rows of fragile upside-down tea cups, stacks of their matching saucers. All in a rose pattern of pale pink and green.

And besides all that? A sparkling crystal forest of barware and stemware.

No place to take off a jacket.

Maybe the hat.

But an image of his raised elbow clipping a field of wineglasses gave him pause. Reminded him of a comical bay window scene where a woman wrestled a Christmas tree.

Instead, he devised an entirely different plan.

He switched off the light. Pocketed the phone.

Then he shoved open that creaking door.

Lunged into the shadowy twilight.

And dove for the cover of the kitchen island.

THREE

ANNA GAZED at the nearest line of large windows through the kitchen's growing darkness. Through their wavy leaded glass. Toward a sky dimmed to a slate gray by fading twilight.

She wondered if anyone could see in through those windows. See her. A trespasser in a forbidden room.

Another low thump resonated.

Then a fast creak.

She froze.

Had that been... in the kitchen with her?

Behind her?

Or in the adjoining dining room? The only room she hadn't investigated.

Exhaling a slow breath through pursed lips, she waited. Listening.

The instrumental Christmas music continued playing in the distant background. Between the muted murmurs of the tour group. Both somewhere upstairs.

Eventually she drew in a deep breath and turned,

shaking off the feeling of someone nearby. Certain her imagination had begun to play with her mind.

Because no further thuds sounded. And no other nearby floorboards creaked.

Still.

She remained on guard. While she surveyed the well-appointed square kitchen, which occupied the entire back corner of the house.

Velvety gray soapstone counters stretched over rosewood cabinetry, including a sizable workspace island. The walls had been painted a functional buttercream semigloss. A stainless steel six-burner stove with two oven doors, commercial dishwasher, white apron sink, and double-door refrigerator fringed the perimeter.

None of that original.

Very little appeared to be.

Likely the hardwood flooring had been. Maybe the sculptural sink fixtures. Possibly the retrofitted light fixtures. She knew the Queen Anne had been originally built with electrical and indoor plumbing—one of the first in town in 1896—but even those back-in-the-day luxuries had been updated during the extensive kitchen remodel. Evidenced by GFCI outlets.

Probably why the official tour she'd taken, two days ago, hadn't included the kitchen. And three nights ago, the kitchen had bustled for a charity event, where she'd been a plus-one.

While she assessed the kitchen, the hairs on the back of her neck stood on end. Some sixth sense getting triggered. As if someone spied on her.

From the far side of the kitchen? Its opposite corner featured two mystery doors. The one in the center of the

outer wall likely led outside. The other, toward the corner...
she had no idea. The dining room, maybe.

The kitchen was dark. And growing darker. Gaining
creeping shadows.

And that dying twilight cast only a miniscule glow.
Through the kitchen's eight lead glass windows. Six along
her left, above the counters. Two on the far side, beside
those two far doors.

None of the retrofitted light fixtures—the chandelier
hanging above the island and four evenly spaced sconces
along the walls—were on.

And she didn't dare spotlight herself with the flip of a
light switch.

Another tiny creak, nearby, prickled fear down her
spine.

Dammit!

She pinched her eyes closed, shallowed her breaths, and
listened.

Muted footfalls reverberated through the overhead floorboards: The tour still made their rounds up on the second floor.

Nothing else.

No other presence materialized.

She snorted and opened her eyes.

And remained the only person standing there.

"You're imagining things," she muttered.

Or upsetting kitchen ghosts.

Probably just hearing the usual creaks and groans of an
ancient house reacting to a touring herd.

After a slight headshake to clear out the heebie-jeebies,
she sucked in a deep breath, squared her shoulders, then
soldiered on.

Back to the plan.

She strode around the corner of the kitchen island to examine its drawers and cabinets, confident in her sanity and tight on time. *Five minutes.* More or less.

A little behind schedule. But doable.

Fingertips balanced atop a brass pull, she tugged a wide shallow top drawer open, nice and slow. And discovered a stocked utensil drawer. A deeper drawer below held even more: sets of measuring cups and spoons, peelers and zesters, two metal whisks, three glass liquid measures, and several nested strainers. A cabinet, right beside the drawers, revealed a pale blue Kitchenaid mixer parked beside assorted glass nesting bowls.

She spun around, opening the tall pantry to the left of the refrigerator. Revealing all manner of mason jars filled with sundry baking ingredients: flours, sugars, salts, spices.

A deep clunk sounded.

She shot a glance up toward the white ceiling, listening.

Had that come from farther away? From downstairs? Or up above?

A quick rhythmic series of thuds resonated.

Yet even with all her focus, she couldn't pinpoint from where.

Seemed like all different directions.

Panic speared through her, quickening her pulse.

As the possibilities of those latest sounds raced through her mind.

A lone tourist jogging down the stairs? Someone dropping a phone? No. Not with that bouncing rhythm. Maybe a rubber ball. Even though no kids were on the tour?

No. None of that made sense.

And by the scuffling muted thuds, the tour still remained upstairs.

But not for long.

She needed to get out of the kitchen. Only one door in or out. Besides those two far mystery doors.

But first, she had one more thing to check.

She turned right, facing the refrigerator.

Its double doors were ivory enameled, made to look vintage. It sat to the right of two really cool wooden doors with metal hinges: an original icebox. The investigation of which had to wait till later.

She pulled the wide double refrigerator doors open.

Which bathed bright light into the dark kitchen. And spiked additional fear into her. Of who might see in through those leaded windows. How she might get caught.

Only a few essentials sat on the bare glass shelves. Nonperishables and other ingredients left over from the holiday events. Half a dozen boxes of unsalted butter. Four eighteen-count cartons of eggs. Numerous jars of different pickles and olives. Rounds and wedges of various cheeses.

All told, with the pantry items?

Enough to work with.

Stage three. Reconnoiter the kitchen, unseen. Check.

After a satisfied nod, she gave a slight smile. Then closed the doors. Casting the kitchen into near-darkness again.

Except...

A darker shadow hovered, to her immediate right.

One that hadn't been there before.

A large... *man.*

She started with a gasp, nearly jumping out of her skin.

Perfect. Not unseen at all.

Plan? Foiled.

FOUR

JONATHAN'S HEART RACED. That he'd finally stood out in the open. Announced his presence.

To a most intriguing mystery woman. Who'd seemed hellbent on not getting noticed.

However, the woman—who'd earlier crept through the house, hyperaware of her surroundings—had been so absorbed by the boring contents of the refrigerator, he'd been able to stroll up through the kitchen behind her.

And she hadn't even noticed.

Not even when a floorboard had creaked.

Or with the air-current change, when he'd stepped behind the door she held.

What was so mesmerizing about food in a refrigerator?

During the couple of minutes prior, after his noisy dive from the china closet, he'd hidden behind the kitchen island. Had even thought he'd been made, when she'd stepped halfway down, toward his end.

But then, all she'd done was pull open a couple of drawers. And a cabinet.

Staying on his hands and knees, he'd peered around the island's corner.

While she'd opened the far pantry, examining its contents.

Like she'd done with the refrigerator.

As if she'd been casing the place.

Which made no sense at all. In a kitchen.

Now that he'd stepped into her clear line of sight, he stared down at her, taking in her facial features for the first time. Which were softened in the gray glow of twilight.

A thick curtain of dark brown bangs fringed the slender tips of her arching brows. Longer hair framed a delicate heart-shaped face. Caramel skin flushed pink over high cheekbones.

And her pert nose wrinkled over a developing frown.

She smelled amazing. Sweet and spicy, like a cinnamon sugar cookie.

"Raiding the fridge?" he murmured. No idea what else to say.

Dark eyes narrowed at him. "What are you, the nosy tiptoeing fridge police?" she whispered in clipped fierceness.

Tension roiled off her body.

Why?

Because he'd interrupted her? While she'd been... taking inventory?

He tilted his head, holding her gaze. "*Who* are you, the nosy tiptoeing fridge police." Yeah. He couldn't help the correction. Or stoking her riled temper.

"Oh. My mistake." She rolled her eyes. "It's the grammar police."

Pegged. Straight on. And not a damn thing wrong with that.

He arched his brows at her. "And who are you?"

"*None* of your business," she hissed. "Go. Away."

"Sorry, can't. I've caught a beautiful Latina cat burglar."

"Great." She crossed her arms, narrowing her eyes again, then huffed out a sigh. "Trouble."

Oh, yeah, he was. In more ways than she realized.

Muffled stomps reverberated on the overhead floor joists.

She winced, glanced up, then began to chew on the corner of her lower lip.

Her breaths shallowed. She tensed her folded arms, then drummed the fingertips of her right hand on her biceps.

A toned biceps, he deduced. Because she wore fitted clothes over a proportioned frame. A navy knit sweater over a gray turtleneck. Darker gray corduroys. Expensive black zero-drop boots. All soft and worn but well-maintained. Providing form and function over style.

She arrowed a glare at him. "What are you doing here? You weren't on the tour."

He snorted, amused at Little Miss Lost-in-the-Fridge. "How do you know?"

A stiff forefinger slammed up against her lips. Her brows shot down.

His brows crept up, at the silent reprimand.

Apparently, his voice had risen. Matching his disbelief.

He gave a slight nod: He'd be quiet. Keep her cover from getting blown.

"I'd have noticed," she muttered.

Unexpected pride flared through his chest. That she felt he would've made such a memorable impression.

"What are you doing here?" She stared hard at him, searching his eyes.

To see if the two of them were cut from the same cloth?

Wondering if he could be trusted?

"Same as you, I guess," he murmured with a shrug. "Bored over semester break."

"No. I meant *here*," she whispered. "In the kitchen. Not on the tour."

He stepped closer, wanting to honor her demand to keep the noise down. And just wanting to get closer.

She edged a little backward.

But he edged a little forward, keeping their closeness, insisting on the intimacy.

"You were sneaking around, avoiding them," he murmured, staring into her dark widening eyes. "So I snuck too, tailing you. *Way* better tour."

She swallowed hard, staring up at him.

But she held her ground, squaring her shoulders, hiking her chin. "This *isn't* a tour."

"Good. I'm not a tourist."

"Great," she grumbled. "A mouthy comedian."

The stomping above got louder.

More rhythmic.

And held greater volume.

As if the entire group took long purposeful strides.

Panic shot through her widening eyes, and she sucked in a deep breath.

While she stared at him.

As if he held her fate in his hands.

And he did.

"Come on." He slipped his hand in hers, then spun her around. "We only have a few seconds to hide."

The surprised look on her face almost made him laugh.

But a hard squeeze from her hand told him that everything rode on the next few seconds.

And that she trusted him.
For now.

FIVE

"STUCK IN A CLOSET AGAIN," the guy muttered, rustling the side of Anna's hair with his warm breath.

A guy who smelled really nice. Of nature and the earth, like clay, minerals, and pine.

"Again?"

They'd been stuck under the stairs for a good ten minutes. In total silence. Other than the soft rasping of their breaths. And the pulse hammering at her eardrum, just beginning to calm. From one of a frightened rabbit. Into something more like crushing schoolgirl.

He was attractive. From what little she gleaned from a minute and a half in a shadowy kitchen. Broad shouldered. Dark featured. Sarcastic humor.

"Second time in a closet," he murmured. "Both because of you."

Oh. Maybe that second door in the far corner of the kitchen. Which explained half the creaky groans she'd heard.

"Not sure this counts as a closet. More like a crawlspace." Cramped. In total darkness. Both of them wedged in. Knees shoved to their chests, legs tangled, backs curved.

His lips hovered close to hers. Really close.

And with every breath he inhaled and exhaled, a slight crinkling sounded. From his bright yellow puffer jacket.

"Think it's safe to come out now?" he asked.

"Let's wait. Just a little longer." Another cramped minute? Could make all the difference.

They'd raced from the kitchen right as shoes began to descend the stairs.

Without pausing to stop, he'd tugged her through the central hall, then jabbed a finger through a clever knothole in the wood paneling under the stairs.

He'd crouched in first, barely fitting. Right as the leading shoes on the stairs went from shins, to knees, to thighs.

Then, with a tug, he'd guided her down beside him and pulled the paneling closed.

Before any faces appeared on the staircase. Narrowly escaping eye contact.

And as the minutes had dragged by, the sounds diminished. Then had ceased altogether.

"Okay." She exhaled a deep breath. "I think we're good now."

Twelve minutes stuffed into a crawlspace. Five after the last sounds, which she suspected had been the docent closing the front door.

With a shift and a shove, he popped open the paneling.

And then in the reverse of how he'd guided her in, he helped push her up and out.

With her entire left side asleep, all pins and needles as blood flow returned, she nearly stumbled as she took a step into the shadowy hall. Faint light—from the still-lit

Christmas tree in the bay window of the parlor—enabled her to see in the darkness.

"Uh, a little help?" He reached up a hand.

She wrapped both hands around his larger one, then tugged backward, helping him unfold what had to be a six-foot frame out of the crawlspace.

He *did* stumble forward. Right into her arms.

Making her stumble several steps backward, holding on tight, trying to prevent their fall.

Then they stood there. In the shadowy hall.

Breaths shallowing, heart racing, she stared up at him.

He took a deep breath. Licked his lips. Quirked a half smile down at her.

"I'm Jonathan, by the way," he murmured.

"Anna."

First name basis. After the intimacy of being on top of one another. In total silence.

While a bazillion thoughts had raced through her mind. At first, fueled by the fear of discovery. But then, all about the man who'd hidden her away.

A man who had become a willing accomplice.

And an unexpected complication.

"Nice to finally meet you, Anna."

His head began to lower, his dark eyes softening.

Her heart hammered double-time.

In a weak moment of insanity, she almost let the kiss happen.

But then she squeezed his biceps, ducked down a few inches, then broke out of their embrace by taking a giant step backward.

Her gaze snagged on a dried dark gash and a bump at his hairline. "Oh, wow." She ran a gentle finger over the bump.

He winched at the touch.

Frowning, she stared into both of his eyes. Angled his face toward the ambient light, with a finger on his chin. But gave a nod when the pupils seemed normal, as far as she could tell. Matching. Both blown wide in the near-darkness.

"You need to go now." She needed to get on with her plan.

He coughed out a laugh, amusement sparkling in his eyes. "I'm going nowhere."

"But..." She had a mission to carry out.

"But nothing." He folded his arms, narrowing his eyes. "I didn't follow you, then hide with you, just to leave. Not now. Not after"—he pointed a forefinger back and forth between their chests—"*this*."

Yep. *Trouble.* The most dangerous kind: determined flirty college guy.

"Great." Maybe she could convince him to leave somewhere along the way.

"Oh, *nooo...*" He took a step toward her, gave a severe headshake.

"What?" She frowned.

"You are *not* getting rid of me."

"How..." *Do you read minds?*

"I know that scheming look. I have two older sisters. I'm well acquainted with all kinds of ditching tricks."

Fine. She arched a brow at him. "And how acquainted are you with baking?"

Because he either needed to get busy, or get out.

He gave a heavy blink. Then his brows arched and the corners of his lips twitched. "Better than you, I'd wager."

SIX

TWENTY MINUTES LATER, Jonathan crossed his ankles on the queen bed in the largest upstairs bedroom, looking forward to the unexpected adventure of Anna.

She had just huffed out a frustrated sigh.

He pressed his lips together, working hard not to smile. Or laugh.

They'd just settled onto the bed. Shoulder to shoulder. Legs outstretched. Backs leaning against two fluffy rows of pillows.

On top of the white quilt.

His jacket and hat had been parked on the front hall coatrack, downstairs. Their shoes on the floor, tucked under either side of the bed.

The generous bedroom had a full-size Christmas tree in the far corner, decorated in silver, red, and green, with white lights. Beside two pink-upholstered wing chairs. With a colorful Tiffany lamp on a lace-covered table in between.

To their left hung a large beveled mirror. Mounted in an ivory frame with pink flowers painted at the top. Centered between two larger windows covered by white lace curtains.

He'd insisted they camp out in the bedroom.

Because immediately after they'd sprung themselves from the crawlspace, she'd led him back into the kitchen. Then had stared at the line of windows, and out into the darkening night.

While she'd worried that lower lip again.

How well do you think someone can see through those windows? she'd asked.

Well enough to get caught, he'd answered.

Which meant they had an entire night to kill. Because no way in hell were they lighting up that kitchen at night.

"*Why* are we watching this?" She drummed impatient fingers on her corduroys.

"*Because* it's an awesome baking show."

She had revealed very little of her mystery plan. Had only told him her motivation behind all the sneaking. And the staying. That she lived in a dorm, had no "home" to go home to over semester break, and wanted to bake in a kitchen.

Which seemed like a flimsy justification for such extreme measures.

She exhaled another exasperated sigh. "I already know how to bake cookies."

"Cookies." Exactly his point. "This is *The Great British Baking Show*. They don't do cookies. And I can't believe you've never watched this. What kind of baker are you?"

"The *cookie* baking kind."

"Well, we've got an entire Christmas Eve Eve to kill. Might as well watch baking."

"Christmas Eve Eve..." she parroted, sticking out a pouty lower lip. Which had protruded for the last fifteen minutes, while he'd gotten them somewhere semi-comfortable for the night.

Made him want to lean over and kiss her senseless.

Suck that plump lower lip of hers.

Make that adorable pout disappear.

Give her something else to dwell on besides delayed cookie-baking plans.

"Yeah." He held his phone up on the pillow propped between them, the Netflix app all cued up. "*The night before* the night before Christmas. Christmas Eve Eve."

"Hm." She crossed her arms and dropped them onto her chest with a hard jerk. Unconvinced. Unimpressed. Unashamed.

And he loved every minute of her refreshing feistiness.

"Besides"—he glanced at her—"these are holiday editions."

He tapped a finger on the play icon. And the show's catchy theme music rolled.

In silence, they watched the first challenge of the first episode: holiday cake pops.

But at the start of the second challenge's sausage roll wreaths, she leaned forward. Staring with rapt attention. Clearly hooked.

Then the third challenge started to roll. "Okay. You have your pick."

Her brow twitched down. "Pick of what?"

"What we're going to compete on."

"Compete." She shot him a sideways glance.

"Compete."

She tapped a finger to the screen, pausing the show. "You and me."

"Unless you want to drag some other poor souls into this."

"No." She tapped play. "Just you."

"So, you have your pick. This one is gingerbread houses: option number one. So pay close attention."

And she did, as the gingerbread challenge baked on.

She gave a slight headshake halfway through. "No way could I do anything that elaborate."

"Says the cat burglar."

She remained quiet for the remaining final minutes as the bakers assembled their showstopper gingerbread houses.

"Wow." Her expression grew dubious as they added all the details to their pieces.

"Right?" Impressive.

And he'd had a hunch Little Miss Lost-in-the-Fridge would love the baking show.

"What's option number two?"

"We'll watch that challenge next." No big deal skipping around. They had all night.

When her other option began streaming, she snorted. "Yule logs."

"As simple or elaborate as you want." A blast, either way.

"There is no part of *that*"—she tapped a fingernail over a chocolate-slathered swirl of dark sponge and white cream —"that's simple."

"I dunno." He glanced at her. "Could be *funnn...*"

"That kitchen would be a disaster zone."

Exactly. "You're making my point for me."

After the Yule logs challenge ended, he switched to the holiday episode featuring the cast from *Derry Girls*.

Anna squealed with delight. Clearly a fan of *that* show.

Seemed appropriate.

Misfit delinquents baking.

Once her home-girl episode finished, she grew somber

through the end music and credits. "Do you think the penalty will be severe... if we're caught?"

"You mean, what will we be charged with *if we're arrested*?"

She frowned. "Well, you don't have to make it sound so bad."

"Bad being... realistic?" She had to have thought of the consequences.

"What are we guilty of?"

He shrugged. "Breaking and entering."

"But nothing was broken."

"Yet." And from their point of view.

"Ever."

He deadpanned her.

"No breaking," she insisted.

He arched his brows. She had a point. Technically the house had been open wide. Conducting a tour.

They'd just gone off format. And way off the schedule. "Just entering, then."

"Trespassing," she countered.

He glanced at her. "For sure."

And yet, all they were doing at the moment was lying on a bed.

Watching holidays editions of *The Great British Baking Show*.

All the rest of it?

That was what had him worried.

And... intrigued.

SEVEN

BLINDING light streamed straight into Anna's eyes as she blinked them open.

Bright *sunlight*.

She had fallen fast asleep. During the holiday baking shows.

She remembered an episode with something she'd never heard of before: chocolate stollen wreaths decorated with white icing. *Annnd...* that was it.

Total lights out.

All the way till morning?

Jonathan.

She bolted upright.

And found herself all alone.

Instrumental Christmas music streamed from somewhere down the hall.

She still sat on top of the beautiful white quilt on the queen bed. Except, instead of Jonathan beside her, a wooden breakfast tray rested there. With a silver cover resting over a large plate. A fork had been centered on a white cloth napkin. His phone angled on the tray's lower corner.

She picked up the phone, tapping it on. Arching her brows, surprised it wasn't password protected.

And horrified that she'd slept past ten.

A note appeared on screen:

Hello, beautiful.

Breakfast is served. Coffee is on the nightstand, for safe keeping.

Wolf it all down if you want to help bake.

Fourth double-batch is in the oven, fifth is on deck.

Early Christmas-Eve-bird bakes all the gingerbread men...

∼ Jonathan

p.s. ∼ You talk in your sleep. :)

p.p.s. ∼ Bring the phone down with you.

Oh no. What had she said in her sleep?

Her plans about baking gingerbread men, apparently.

But how much more?

She lifted the plate cover. Steaming scrambled eggs were piled high, topped with dried chives. Two pointy drop biscuits, herbed with aromatic basil, sat beside them.

Famished, she grabbed the fork and shoveled in a mouthful of eggs.

"Mmmm..." Perfect. Buttery. Moist. Salted just right.

How thoughtful. The clever flirty devil.

Yet her heart warmed. That he'd gone to such lengths.

For a girl he'd just met.

Anxious to join him, she chewed and swallowed quickly. She bit into one of the fragrant biscuits. *Delicious.* Crisp on the outside. Soft and olive oily rich inside.

Once she'd polished at least half the food, with decent coffee gulped down in between, she shoved his phone in her pants pocket and put on her boots.

Then she headed down with the tray, half-full coffee mug balanced on top.

"Knock, knock," she said outside the kitchen door, hands gripping both sides of the breakfast tray.

"*Cominggg...*" came the reply.

He opened the door wide enough for her to enter. Then he spun back into the room, rounded the kitchen island, and bent over, focusing.

Flour dusted the right side of his head.

A pointy blue icing bag angled down from his right hand.

And the whole kitchen had been transformed—into a Christmas-baking explosion.

Cooling racks covered nearly every surface, across the kitchen island and the counters under the windows. On the racks, an army of gingerbread men marched, most already iced.

"But... how did you..." She set the breakfast tray on a tiny patch of unoccupied counter near the sink.

He glanced up from finishing a cookie he'd half-iced. A white line of icing stretched from the bag's tip to the gingerbread man's middle button. "I wanted to surprise you."

"You did." Without doubt.

"You said you were worried you wouldn't have enough time to get all the batches done."

"I was." No denying it.

He stuck a forefinger under the bag's tip, removing the icing trail, then licked his finger. "We should have plenty of time."

A flash of heat warmed through her. At how erotic that finger-suck had looked.

"Plenty of time *tooo…*?" How much had she revealed?

And how on board had he gotten?

"To deliver them to the children's home."

Right. She had told him everything. And he'd gone all-in.

"Any room for me in here?" She surveyed the production line, not wanting to mess with his flow.

"Yep." He nodded toward the other side of the island, then finished the man's buttons. He began icing the head. "Saved an entire batch for you. Ingredients are all lined up, beside the mixing bowl."

Right. Ingredients. No recipe. "You planning on helping me?"

He paused in his icing line. Then slowly lifted his gaze.

In the brighter light of morning, his handsome features struck her anew. Black mussed hair. Soulful chestnut-brown eyes. Dusting of freckles over an olive complexion. Strong jawline covered with a couple of days of unshaven scruff.

"I *knew* it," he said.

"Knew what?"

"You've never baked gingerbread cookies before, have you?"

Her cheeks flushed. "No."

All along, she'd thought *How hard could it be? Follow a recipe. Cut out some men.*

Yeah. Total fail.

She'd obviously underestimated the skill involved.

At least, she'd had the foresight to worry about the time commitment. In her sleep.

"Yes." He gave her a warm smile. "I'll be right there."

The warmth of that smile and his kindhearted tone made her stomach flip.

Because the statement felt like so much more. Ran far deeper.

As if Jonathan would be there, right beside her.

Through a whole lot more than just baking cookies.

EIGHT

JONATHAN FED ANNA one of her baked cookies, soft and gooey, hot out of the oven. Feet first.

She closed her full luscious lips around the bite with a low groan, eyes half closing.

Then she took the cookie from him, curved her mouth into a wicked smirk, broke the little guy's head off, and fed it to him.

His chest ached. A deep burning fire. Dead center.

Because standing there in the kitchen, the woman who'd been beautiful in the shadows of twilight, and adorable in the glow of his phone in the bedroom darkness, had become absolutely stunning in the bright light of day.

Every bit of her...

Soulful eyes. Intelligent mind. Daring soul.

Enormous heart.

Before he had a chance to chew, she leaned up on tiptoe and kissed him.

Surprised by her sudden boldness, heat speared through him.

But the real shocker? His heart flipped.

He dropped the icing bag and grabbed her hips.

She tossed the half-eaten man and gripped her fingers into his hair.

And standing in the middle of a kitchen overrun with gingerbread men, with flour and sugar and spices dusting every surface, they embraced with fierce passion, kissed like their life depended on it.

When they finally came up for air, they searched one another's eyes.

Gasping for air.

Hearts racing.

"Sooo..." He had a profound need to know her better. To learn all he could.

And he felt raw. Heart torn wide open. Which made it seem okay to dive deep, going all the way. "Were you a... did you come from... a children's home?"

She swallowed hard. Sucked in a deep breath.

Her eyes began to glitter with unshed tears.

Then she gave a slow nod. "Yeah. Not this one we're bringing the cookies to. But... yeah."

He understood. Sensed her enormous restraint. The tension under the surface. Her struggle with it all.

And he planned to give her whatever space and time she needed.

"It's okay that I helped?" He glanced around at all the work he'd done. And hoped she didn't feel that he'd stolen that from her.

"Of course." She ran her fingers through his hair. Plucked a gingerbread crumb out. Then ate it.

"Okay." He blew out a relieved breath. "Good."

She gave him a slow smile. "But we still get to compete, right?"

"Gingerbread houses? Or Yule logs?"

"Yule logs." She gave a decided nod. "We've still got the place to ourselves."

"All Christmas Day." His family would recover. He had more important things to do.

"But..." She frowned. "What about tonight?"

He drew in a deep breath. Then gave her a tender kiss.

When he eased them apart, he searched her eyes.

Anna wasn't the kind of girl he wanted just for one night.

She was the one he wanted to keep.

A most unexpected Christmas gift: a Robinhood baker in a beautiful package.

"Tonight... we binge watch *The Great British Baking Show*." He arched a brow at her. "*On top* of the quilt." Total gentleman. For the first time ever.

She huffed out a laugh. "There's more *Baking Show*?"

"Over a dozen seasons."

Plenty of PG-rated programming.

For a woman *so* worth stalking, hiding, and trespassing for.

Definitely worth the wait.

EPILOGUE

THEY STOOD in the small parking lot, outside the children's home, under a sunny cloudless sky.

Midafternoon, Christmas Eve.

Anna rested her head on Jonathan's shoulder.

He tightened his arm around her.

And she'd never felt more home than in those moments.

They waited in front of an unassuming main house and neighboring smaller houses. All brick ranch styles with asphalt shingled roofs. Xeriscaped with tan granite walkways between small-leafed plants dusted with a fine layer of snow.

After they'd spent hours more baking and icing, then a mad search through the kitchen, they'd found square cake boxes. Which, with sheets of parchment paper between layers of gingerbread men, worked just fine.

For transporting eight dozen gingerbread men.

And women. She'd insisted on getting some girl-power cookies in there.

They'd had a blast, icing personalities into the later batches.

And on the very last ones, had even made private R-rated versions. Just for them.

But when they'd first arrived at the children's home, Anna had insisted on going in alone. Needed to face it on her own, as a form of therapy. To know that a person could come from a place like that, and not have it define them. Not in any limiting way.

And yet, have it leave a mark on her heart, in all the best ways.

Two of the "home mothers" had come out with wide smiles on their faces. Took the stacks of boxes Jonathan unloaded from his car—which he'd jogged a few blocks home to retrieve.

And after profuse thanks, the women had turned and left, taking the cookies inside while she and Jonathan watched.

She didn't need to personally see the kids faces. Didn't have any ego in it at all.

In fact, she'd snuck into the Queen Anne house more on a lark than anything else.

In her head, she'd had a plan. Make it inside, stake out the place, claim the kitchen. And yet, for all the rest? She had planned on winging it. See how it all unfolded.

Boy had she been surprised.

She glanced up at Jonathan. "You're the best Christmas present I've *ever* gotten."

He stared down at her, wonder in his expression, amusement sparkling in his eyes. "Christmas *Eve* present."

Then he let out a slow sigh, leaned down, and gave her the softest kiss.

He murmured against her lips, "I feel the exact same way..."

"Yeah?"

"Yep." He said between tiny kisses. "I've caught myself a Christmas cat burglar."

She danced small kisses over his mouth, fighting a smile. "And I've trapped myself a master baker... and part-time nosy fridge police."

He rested his forehead on hers. "Yeah, you have."

EXTRA SPECIAL BONUS EPILOGUE

THE FOLLOWING DAY, Anna and Jonathan raced down the stairs, total kids on Christmas morning.

Filled with the brightness of new love in their hearts.

Excited for their very first baking challenge.

They'd almost stayed up all night. Almost.

Except for a handful of early-morning hours when they'd passed out, cuddled in each other's arms. After a marathon *Bake Off*, as the Brits called it.

They'd also asked each other a bazillion questions through the night. And given honest answers.

What were they studying?

Pre-med for her. How she'd known his head bump hadn't caused a concussion.

Forestry for him. Why he'd smelled so amazing, of earth and pine.

How had they landed at the same university?

She'd worked enormously hard, had gotten straight A's in advanced courses, and had landed a full scholarship.

His father happened to be the Dean of the Business

College. Why he'd gone into forestry. Well, that, and he happened to love trees.

Which, he'd said, *made me fall for you the moment you'd plunged elbows-deep into a Christmas tree. As you wrestled to save a falling Fraser fir.*

But none of those things mattered. Not at the moment.

Not when battling it out for the most important title on Christmas Day.

To be crowned Star Baker in their first ever Queen Anne Yule Log Bake Off.

They had set the timer for two hours. If the Brits could do it? So could they.

They had split the kitchen island into two baking territories: her the left, him the right.

Anna had never baked a sponge in her life.

Neither had Jonathan.

But they had a blast giving it a go.

They cheated, of course. Peeking over shoulders when the other wasn't looking.

"Hey." She gave a stern headshake. "No copying."

"Nope. I'm doing a fatless Swiss roll."

"So am I!" She curved and lifted her shoulder, laughing, and trying (but failing) to block his view.

He arched an imperious brow. "Mine is *chocolate*. With hazelnut buttercream. And rum."

"Yeah? Well, mine's gingerbread." Yep. She'd developed a fierce love for all things gingerbread. "With Bailey's buttercream."

Because of their last-minute recipes, they'd had to hit the grocery in the final hours of Christmas Eve. Along with about a dozen other desperate madcap bakers.

And, being the good Samaritan trespassers they were,

they added to their carts all the replacement ingredients to restock the Queen Anne's fridge and pantry.

To ensure that theft couldn't be added to their clear and obvious—but in no way regretted—trespass.

Side by side, with loads of laughter and rampant kissing, they each made their best first Yule logs ever. Together in the main oven, they baked their Swiss sponges. With only one mixer, they took turns whipping up their buttercreams. Her Bailey's Swiss meringue buttercream first.

His hazelnut buttercream second.

"Plus the rum." He splashed some in.

Right as they leaned toward one another, speaking into a silicone spoon-top microphone. Quoting *Bake Off's* Selasi, "Everyone loves a lil' tipple during Christmas."

He stirred up melty dark chocolate ganache.

She made a sweeter white chocolate.

Racing against the clock, they slathered their sponges with their buttercreams, then rolled them up into tight swirls.

Laughing when his timer sounded a five-minute warning, they each gooped their respective ganaches onto their logs. Finesse? Out the window.

Losing the battle, she tossed the spatula across the island, then began spreading white chocolate onto her log with all ten fingers.

Not to be outdone, he ditched his spatula, then smeared on dark chocolate with flattened palms.

She watched the timer hit the last few seconds.

"Three..." she said.

"Two..." he stalked toward her with chocolate covered hands.

"*One!*" They both shouted, as she fled around one side of the kitchen island.

He gave chase, then doubled back, going the opposite direction.

But she just stood there, laughing in surrender, gleefully letting him capture her.

They held on to each other's faces, smearing chocolate all over one another.

The laughter died down when they broke into tiny kisses, small tastings of each other's lips. Then erupted all over again when she licked his chin. And he slurped over hers.

Over slow wonderful seconds, they remained in the sticky joyful embrace, catching their breaths. While they stared into each other's eyes.

He tapped his nose to hers. "Best Christmas break ever," he murmured. "I knew it the moment I saw you."

"Best *first* Christmas break." She gave him a slow heartfelt kiss.

"Deal," he agreed. "The best kind of Christmas tradition. *Ours.*"

❄

BILLIONAIRE BASH NEW YEAR'S CRASH

ONE

HOVERING at the edge of the world's most exclusive New Year's Eve party, Dali sucked in a steadying breath. Attempting to not pass out right then and there. Before she'd even stepped one glittering high heel into the fray.

Cora, her best friend since high school, had somehow conned her into this scheme.

Then they had conned their way into a world so far above them, they'd shot stratospheric.

Into *really* thin air.

Which felt... artic.

She labored to draw in a full inhale in the ballgown. The first gown she'd ever worn. A strapless number spun from fairy tale dreams. With gossamer layers of iridescent violet-green chiffon—woven across her breasts, ruched through a clingy bodice, then billowing in a sheer diaphanous cloud from hips to toes—over a fitted sage-green satin undergown.

Struggling to breathe, due the gown's vertical boning, clamped tight around her ribcage.

While tottering on four-inch heels. Which had a ridiculously thin sparkly green strap across her violet-polished toes.

Who the hell designed these torturous contraptions?

Oh, that's right. Men.

Probably one of the tuxedo-wearing sadists mingling on the main floor below. The main floor of an impressive multi-million-dollar mountain retreat.

She and Cora stood side by side, perched at the end of an elevated slate-tiled entrance hall. They had just arrived. At eleven p.m. on the nose. Dropped off by a black stretch limo, which Cora had insisted upon.

Everything had been orchestrated by Cora to the last detail, including the critical timing. Arrive two hours after the party's start. One hour before midnight.

Just enough time to flirt with wealthy drunk bachelors.

Not so early that they aroused suspicion.

Suspicion Dali planned to avoid. At all costs.

But first, they paused at their entrance to the party, as per the plan. Taking a wise few moments to survey their hunting grounds.

Well, Cora's hunting grounds, as far as Dali was concerned.

Because no matter how fervently Cora believed they'd each snag a billionaire, Dali had zero interest. Which she'd vehemently stated from the beginning, that morning. With half a dozen fabulous ass-protecting reasons.

Yet when Cora had sighed, shoulders slumped, eyes welling with tears, Dali had caved.

In the whirlwind fourteen hours since, especially the last few, as they'd had crazy fun getting dressed up and primped up—in another woman's gowns, in that woman's unoccupied house, based on that woman's party invitation Cora had stolen—Dali had simply nodded.

Cora could afford to delude herself. Could afford to get fired from her luxury-home-sitting gig. She had a dozen more.

Dali had way too much to lose. Had worked hard toward attaining her law degree. Had entered the final homestretch toward graduating.

So Cora could believe what she wanted.

Dali had come for moral support, nothing else.

And if they got caught, Dali planned to plead ignorance.

"Wow," Cora murmured. "This place is stunning."

"Yeah." Dali had never seen such opulence.

At the base of six curving slate-tiled steps stretched a breathtaking series of three rooms, all decorated in dazzling splendor.

In the high corners of the rooms, arrangements of large glowing paper lanterns floated—shimmering in creams, silvers, and golds—hung from thin wires. Strung from chunky timber beams. That spanned under wood-clad angled ceilings.

Down below—against dark floor-to-ceiling windows shining with reflected light—sprawled the generous spaces: a formal dining with two sparkling crystal chandeliers over a long table that offered seating for twenty, a grand central room with towering peaked windows, a more masculine lounge area with a busy stretch of bar, serviced by two hoppin' bartenders.

The three rooms were separated by two dual-sided fireplaces, wide masterpieces whose fieldstones stacked clear up to the rafters, roaring with crackling orange flames.

In the central great room, straight down those six beckoning stairs, two generous conversation areas invited guests to congregate, delineated by Oriental rugs threaded with vivid reds and greens over a dark hardwood floor. Deep ivory slipcovered chairs and sofas, accented by square pillows in pale shades of green and brown, accompanied wooden end tables and cocktail tables.

In the lounge, toward the right, four brown leather club chairs squatted together in front of five matching barrel-shaped barstools tucked against the long bar.

No one sat, though. Not one person.

Everyone mingled, flirted, and drank. Maybe a hundred guests. Mostly white men, wearing black tuxes. About a quarter were white women, many in slinky minidresses. Only a tasteful few wore more elegant full-length gowns.

Several couples danced on open wood flooring in the main room, to bass rhythms that a DJ streamed from a corner in the lounge.

Creating more intimate spaces, tall slender evergreens—decorated with white lights, short ivory ribbons and silver spiraled streamers—gathered together in twos and threes.

Here and there, bouquets of large balloons—silver, gold, ivory, and a few clear filled with silver-and-gold confetti—hovered at the edges of furniture groupings, strings anchored by silver-foiled weights.

Four waitstaff, dressed in all black, worked their way through the guests, a silver serving tray balanced on a palm, offering a variety of hors d'oeuvres.

The home's interior gave off the rustic heavenly scents of cedar and pine.

"Ready?" Cora swept a predatory gaze over her hunting grounds, straightening her shoulders.

Goose bumps broke out over Dali's skin.

And not just from the briskness of the air.

A sudden flash of panic backed her up a step. "No. I can't believe you made me *do* this."

"One night. You can handle it."

"Made me *wear* this." A stolen gown. No matter how beautiful.

"Awww..." Cora turned toward her, shining coppery waves offsetting her creamy skin. A silvery gown shimmering over her willowy frame. "You look amazing. Like an Indian mermaid goddess."

"Great. I look like a mermaid." *Kill me now.*

Cora arrowed a hard stare at her. "Like a *goddess*."

Mm-hmm. A fraud goddess, about to take the plunge into a shark-infested soiree.

"Fine. I'm ready." To get the night over with.

Cora beamed her a bright grateful smile. Then angled a nod toward a group of five men who'd been standing by the windows in the main room, but had turned and headed toward the lounge. "I'm trying those boys. Handsome. Steady on their feet. Alone. Waiting for a brand-new woman to compete over."

The tallest, darkest, broadest of the men shook his head, said something to the others, brow furrowed, then spun around. His companions continued on into the lounge.

Mr. Tall, Dark, and Broad strode through all three rooms, then disappeared past the dining room.

"I'm going for the loner." Not really, but Cora would be none the wiser.

Dali planned to warm herself by the fire. Maybe explore a few of the luxurious rooms. But above all else? She planned to *not* attract attention.

Cora might be planning to catch herself a man.

But the last thing Dali needed? To get caught.

TWO

LOGAN COULDN'T BREATHE. He needed to get out of the house. Away from the party.

Light years away.

For some insane half-second two weeks ago, he had thought hosting an event would be the cure. Yank him back from that dark edge.

Wow, had he been wrong. In so many ways.

Nothing brought family back.

No amount of wealth soothed that gaping wound.

And no superficial celebration would rectify that loss.

The party actually hadn't been his idea. But he'd warmed to it. After a lot of badgering from his four lifelong friends, Thomas, Luke, Bryan, and Coby.

Close as brothers. Thick as thieves.

Well, close until his family's accident.

After that, he'd thrown himself into endless months of seclusion. Isolated from everything. From everyone.

Over the summer, his friends had begun trying to lure him out of the house. Since Thanksgiving, at least one of them had been harassing him every damn day.

And in a moment of weakness, he'd finally agreed.

But not to leave the house.

To change its echoing emptiness. Which had begun to drag him down into a dark abyss.

New Year's Eve, he'd acquiesced. Five drunken hours. How bad could it be?

Turned out... Bad.

Especially when he refused to drink.

Yeah, the guys hadn't counted on that wrinkle.

Logan didn't blame them.

But he didn't have to suffer through the train wreck either.

So when they'd headed back to the bar for their refills, toward the thumping bass music pounding a headache into his brain, he'd excused himself, "I need some air."

Coby had shot him a pointed look.

The guys had all paused, worry etched onto their faces.

But Logan had shaken his head, shaken off their concerns. "Just for a moment."

A convenient half-truth. A blip in time.

Just a handful of compounded moments, over a couple more hours.

And then they'd all be gone.

Until then, what he needed was a quiet escape.

From *The Glamour Party of the Decade!*—themed by the event planner. Lanterns and lights. Sparkle and shimmer. Champagne and caviar.

From dozens of the guys and girls he'd known most of his life.

From the haunting memories and empty house underneath all the decoration.

Sights on the calm darkness at the far end of the house, he ran a hand through his hair and strode through the great room. Not making eye contact with anyone. Glad to leave the stifling heat from those roaring fireplaces.

He tore through the dining room, squinting at the chandeliers' blinding glare.

Barreled through the kitchen, past bustling caterers and harried waitstaff.

And with every next stride toward his bedroom, that thumping bass that pounded the inside of his skull began to fade.

Leather heels clicking on the long corridor's marble floor sounded his successful retreat.

Shadows under an unlit barreled-ceiling quieted his mind.

The darker recesses of his enormous bedroom welcomed him home.

He closed the mahogany double doors, muffling sounds of the party into the far distance.

After a moment, his eyes adjusted to the darkness. Registered the king bed spanning to his left, piled high with perfect ivory bedding. The pair of gray wingchairs and chess table in the sitting room. Large black marble fireplace on the far wall. Pitch-black doorway leading to the giant bathroom beyond.

A place he'd redecorated, made into his own lair. The one thing he'd changed.

Too bad the rest of the world hadn't changed.

Same friends. Same women. Same nonsense.

None of it real. Not anymore.

He sighed, then gravitated toward the wall of windows. Stared out into a moonless night.

Still sweltering from the party, he tugged his bowtie apart and unbuttoned his collar, walking toward the back door. He stepped out onto the terrace.

Brisk December air rushed over his skin. Crisped into his lungs on a deep inhale.

Scents of sweet pine and fresh snow, from a million acres of wintry forest, blew through on a gentle breeze.

The sounds of the party grew more distant, muted through triple-pane windows.

Peace and quiet.

At least he had plenty of that living on forty acres on the top of a mountain.

If only he could figure out where he fit in the lonely new world he'd found himself in. New Year's party? Not the solution.

But if not his old friends, if not the social circles he knew well, then what?

All of a sudden, the sounds of the party amplified. Thumping bass music blared out. Conversations. Laughter. As if the great room's back door had been opened.

Yet instead of the sound diminishing, the door closing, the loudness continued.

He wandered toward the screening barrier between the adjoining balconies—three tall planters with spiraling topiaries strung with white lights—and peered through the plants.

Unable to believe his eyes, he stared, jaw falling open.

A beautiful woman stood at the terrace threshold.

A gentle winter breeze flowed against her. Rippled long dark hair off a caramel face and shoulders. Ruffled shimmering panels of purple-green chiffon against a shapely body.

But it wasn't her beauty or figure that captivated him.

It was her expression. A moment of pure bliss.

Face tilted up toward the night sky. Dark-lashed eyes closed. Full lips parted.

Breathe. He had to remind himself.

Right as the delicate curves of her chest began to expand.

They drew in the same snowy pine air.

And for the first time in almost a year, he wanted something.

Or rather some*one.*

Her.

THREE

OVERHEATED, from the roaring fireplaces and rampant masculine energy vibrating through the extravagant house, Dali stood in a back terrace doorway, escape on her mind.

As she inhaled the most amazing air in the world. Mountain air.

Scented by an enormous pine forest.

The mineral tang of a pending snowstorm.

And maybe a little magic.

How she'd always felt in the mountains. Since she was a little kid.

Why she planned to dedicate her life to protecting it.

The reason she had so much to lose.

If she got caught.

Knowing the danger to blowing her cover existed inside the house, she fully stepped outside and closed the door.

Hushed silence enveloped her.

She gusted out a weary sigh of relief.

What had drawn her through the house's great room in the first place had been curiosity about all the short ivory ribbons on the slender trees by the windows. Many had scripty black writing on them. Of varying lengths. Quotes? Sayings? Messages?

But before she'd had a chance to examine the ribbons, she had to suffer through running the gauntlet of a shark-infested room.

Five separate men had approached in turns, hitting on her. Some bearing drinks. Others dropping a pickup line. All drunk. None of interest.

And trying to extricate herself from the first couple of attempts, she'd back up so close to one fireplace, she'd worried the flowing chiffon panels of her *borrowed* gown would catch fire. With the last three determined men, she'd edged closer to the other fireplace.

Desperate to jump out of the entire fiery cauldron of danger, she'd bolted for the windows as soon as she spotted a back door.

But on her way out, staring through the glass, she'd gotten distracted. By what stretched beyond the windows. Out on the terrace.

An enchanting garden.

A blessedly *empty* garden. Not one sharky man (or woman) in sight.

Marvelous wintry air soothed over her skin. Even as the warmth from a tall cylindrical heater, one of many placed thoughtfully throughout the space, kept the atmosphere pleasant.

She stepped forward into the delightful garden, aching to explore.

Dozens of tall cement pots held manicured evergreen topiaries strung with white lights. The central ones—all skinny, conical, and tall—were spaced several feet apart and formed a diamond lattice pattern over the terrace's large gray slate tiles. On each of the far sides of the garden, a trio of larger spiraling topiaries formed lit screening walls of foliage.

A wide squat fountain, shaped like a four-leafed clover, burbled in the center of the garden. Soft blue-green lights glowing up from underwater. The fountain had a green patina and featured sculptured lily pads near the center and pussy willows sprouting along its back edge. Tiny white petals slow-swirled, floating on the water's surface.

Up above, latticed overhead, draped fluffy garlands of vibrant flowers: snowy white roses tucked into evergreen boughs, dripping with the pale purple haze of wisteria. Strung white lights peeked out between the blossoms.

Wrought iron benches, with ivory cushions and pale purple pillows tucked into each armed corner, curved between several of the potted plants.

And hovering near the far edge of the terrace, beside a see-through cable railing, a wrought iron bistro set beckoned. On its small table-for-two, a flickering tealight floated in a shimmering low glass bowl.

Beyond that see-through railing? Total darkness.

But there had to be a breathtaking view beyond that railing. Because the palatial house, with all its expansive windows, demanded it.

"Like it?" asked a deep bass voice.

She started. Then turned to her left and edged forward to peek around a slender conical topiary beside the fountain.

Through the far end of the spiraled topiary wall, a dark shape stepped into full view.

A man in a tuxedo.

Black hair surrounding his handsome face had grown just long enough to curl. And appeared tousled, like he'd raked a hand through it. And on that striking face, shadowy scruff lined full lips and a strong jawline.

His black silk bowtie had been tugged apart.

The top button of his white shirt was undone.

Mr. Tall, Dark, and Broad.

And oh, *wow*. So *very* sexy. In a primal way.

Undeniable chemistry sparked from him, between them. Washing a wave of heat through her.

Great. She huffed out a frustrated breath.

"Sorry," he said. "Didn't mean to startle you."

Dark eyes held her gaze as he took a long-legged step forward.

"You didn't." She gave a half-shoulder shrug, holding her ground.

Those eyes narrowed as he eased closer. "Yeah, I did."

"Well, yes..." Her pulse quickened. In attraction, for sure. But also in panic, about getting cornered... of getting caught. "But I'm fine."

"You never answered my question." He casually dropped his hands into his trouser pockets, then tilted his head a fraction.

"Question," she repeated, mind blanking.

He took a smaller step forward. Stopped an arm's length from her. "Do you like it?"

Breaths shallowing, she swallowed hard, then glanced up and around her. "The garden?"

"My house."

"This"—she blinked, then glanced through the wall of windows, the luxury throughout—"is *your* house?"

"Yes." He lowered his head a little as she glanced back up at him. "And I'm dying to know... *Who* are *you?*"

FOUR

WITH ONLY A HANDFUL of minutes left of the worst year of his life, in a surprising turn of events, Logan stared down at the most incredible woman he'd ever encountered.

As sheer panic flashed across her face.

Which speared regret through his heart.

That he had somehow frightened the captivating creature who'd wandered into his world.

One who, minutes ago, had been experiencing a clear state of bliss.

While he'd been hidden. A mere voyeur.

Until he'd crashed into her private moment. Unable to stop himself.

But had he come on too strong? More aggressive than she was used too?

It appeared that she'd been lured by the winter garden.

A garden he now loved.

Thank God for Maurice, the event planner. The renowned designer who'd had the foresight—had insisted—on installing a breathtaking garden on the terrace.

You never know who wants to frolic in a garden for a

special moment, Maurice had said. *And the best party? Happens in a single stolen moment.*

Yet Logan wanted more than a stolen moment with the natural beauty before him.

The gentle breeze ruffled wisps of black silky hair around her delicate heart-shaped face. A peachy pink blush flushed the caramel skin over high cheekbones. Thick dark lashes blinked over black wide eyes.

A hint of pale pink gloss shimmered over full lips.

And standing so close to her, the faint scent of vanilla wafted between them.

For the first time in forever, he found he couldn't breathe. Felt excitement vibrate through him. Like a kid on Christmas Eve.

Except he stood there all grown up. On New Year's Eve. In front of his dream girl.

Dream *woman*. As if magically sprouted from the garden itself, wearing a gossamer gown of shimmering purple and green.

Maybe the party hadn't been a mistake after all.

Those thick dark lashes blinked. "Who am I?"

Hands still tucked into his pockets, he backed up a slow step. Giving her a bit more space. "Yes." He gave a small nod, arched his brows, hoping she'd relax a little.

"I'm Dali."

"It's a *pleasure* to meet you, Dali." He held out a hand. "I'm Logan."

She didn't even glance at his hand, crossed her arms instead. Gave him a small nod back. "Hi, Logan."

He curled his fingers inward, then pocketed the hand again. Willing to be patient.

"It's just..."—he gave a bewildered headshake—"*how* have I not met you till now?"

"Oh." Relief washed over her. "We just got here."

We. Damn. She was with someone, then. "Who did you come with?"

He stared into the house, searching the brightly lit rooms. For whatever guy (or girl) had the honor of accompanying her. His competition.

But instead of answering him, she turned and wandered off, toward the windows.

He interpreted that as an invitation to stroll and talk, so he remained right beside her. For conversational sake.

They stopped a few feet from the glass.

Through their reflection, she cast him a nervous glance.

It made him wonder why all the anxiety? Did she have something important to hide? Or an immediate problem she needed to solve?

Which made him want to fix whatever ailed her. In order to bring her bliss back.

He held her gaze in their reflection. "Whatever you're concerned about, there's no need to worry."

Surprise flashed over her delicate features. "There isn't?"

"Nope."

"Oh." Her slender brows furrowed a little.

"Whoever you came with will just have to yield."

She blinked. "Yield?"

"To me." Simple. "I'm taking over now."

"You are?" At that, she turned toward him. "What *exactly* are you taking over?"

He turned toward her, staring into those dark fascinating eyes. "I'm taking over as your escort. For the party."

The corners of her lips twitched. "Escort."

"With gentleman's manners, the whole time."

A small smile curved her lips. She gave a slight nod. "Okay. I accept."

"And I promise, whatever you decide to share, your secret's safe with me."

She turned her head a fraction. "Safe."

"No repercussions."

Her brows arched. "None?"

"None whatsoever."

Because gut instinct told him Dali had layers. Deep layers.

And he wanted to be the lucky one—the only one—to unravel them.

FIVE

DALI STARED up into beautiful darkened eyes. That were a deep vivid green. And sparked with warmth.

No repercussions?

Could she trust Logan?

Did she dare?

No. Too much to lose.

The guy *owned* the palatial home.

Which meant he had money.

And power.

Standing there in what was no doubt a bespoke tuxedo. Fit like a glove. Luxurious black worsted wool. Hint of shine on the peaked satin lapels.

And the appealing rebelliousness of the undone bowtie and the collar button.

Hmmm... No harm in flirting a little. Maybe revealing a tidbit of truth.

Perhaps have some kind of amusing conversation. To pass the time.

While stuck at a party she'd crashed, stuffed into a corseted dress and tottering heels that she'd stol— *borrowed*.

His lips quirked up at the corners. Emphasizing the lovely scruff around them and up that strong jawline.

She inhaled a deep breath.

And wow, he smelled divine. Earthy. Spicy. An attractive hint of masculine musk.

"Okay," she murmured.

"Okay?" He arched thick dark brows.

"Okay." She'd play along. Give him a morsel or two.

She turned toward the glass. Then strolled along it, viewing the party from the safety of the fragrant terrace garden. With her gentlemanly "escort" by her side.

Their vantage from the darkness outside made it feel as if they watched a large aquarium. Apart from the environment. Watching the antics of all the creatures inside.

Including the sharks.

Funny she hadn't thought of Logan as a shark.

And yet, maybe he was the most dangerous of them all.

"There." She nodded toward the group of five in the lounge. One siren. Surrounded by a pack of circling great whites. "The redhead in the silver gown. That's my friend, Cora."

"Friend?" Doubt vibrated through his tone.

"Yes." She glanced up at him.

"Not *date*."

Amused, she fought a smile. "*Not* my date. Cora's got her sights on one of those sharks."

"Sharks." He turned toward the group, huffing out a laugh. "Your term or hers?"

"Mine." No doubt about it. "Your house is full of them."

"True." He rocked forward onto his toes, then back again. "But what makes you think they're sharks?"

"Look at them. Circling their next meal. Going in for a

giant bite, without knowing what's in front of them. They're the great big bad, ready to rip and shred, then spit it out if they don't like it."

"Interesting." He pursed his lips. "Quite the well-formed opinion."

A twinge of panic flashed through her. "You said 'no repercussions.'"

He gave a nod. "And I stand by it."

"Good." Relief relaxed through her shoulders.

"So who do you have your sights on?"

"No one." No thanks.

"You're kidding." His tone dropped. His expression deadpanned.

"No." She frowned. "Why?"

His gaze traveled down her body, then crept back up to level with hers.

For long seconds, he searched her eyes. Indecision warring in his.

Then he gave a slight headshake. "Never mind. You're not ready to share that deep."

"I'm not?" She wasn't. But how did he know?

"Nope. Not till we've had a drink."

"I don't drink."

That deadpan hit her again. Then he gave a slight headshake.

As if he couldn't believe it.

As if he had lots of things—deep things—he held close to his chest too.

"What?" She knew she didn't deserve sincerity. But couldn't help wondering.

"No." His expression hardened. "*Also* not till we've had a drink. A *nonalcoholic* drink. You game for hot chocolate?"

Warmth bloomed in her chest. At his words. His tone. And just... something about him. At *everything* about him.

Which she found a little terrifying.

And... a lot intriguing.

SIX

LOGAN DREW IN A DEEP BREATH. Stared into Dali's beautiful dark eyes. Waiting for her answer.

Scared to death she might say yes.

Yet at the same time, wanting her to. Needing her to. More than anything.

The time had come for him to join the world again.

And in that stolen moment, in the winter garden, made just for that night—for her, as far as he was concerned—hope flared to life in his heart.

But every bit of it hinged on her.

The woman he'd never seen before. The guest of a woman he didn't know.

Two party crashers. Arrived at the eleventh hour. Literally.

Maybe sent from above.

As if angels had a hand in it. Which shocked the hell out of him.

All this time, he had suffered from serious survivor's guilt. Hating all the trappings of wealth. Certain he'd been undeserving. Wishing he could trade it all for realness. For love.

Could Dali be that possibility? Might her stumbling into his world be no coincidence?

He couldn't wait to find out. To unravel those delicate layers.

Whenever she felt ready. However long it took.

Because as someone who'd had to walk his own lonely path, he understood. Being real? Especially with one's self? Took time.

To his eternal relief, she licked her lips, then gave a little nod. "I'd *love* a hot chocolate."

"Great." He extended a hand to her.

She stared at it a beat, then accepted it.

Soft fingers slid over his. Surprisingly warm, given that she wore a strapless gown.

He clasped her hand, holding on tight. But not too tight.

When he turned, she angled toward the great room door.

He shook his head, tugging her onward. "Not through there. I don't want to go back in."

She let out a soft laugh. "To your own party?"

Yeah. Too much of the same. *Not* amazing her. And he wanted to keep their stolen moment private, all to themselves.

Way too much info to unload on her. "Better just the two of us. We'll sneak into the kitchen through the back."

He led her through the spiral topiaries, onto his private terrace, then in through the door.

"This is the back?" She swept a gaze through the darkness while he eased the door closed. "It feels like a bedroom."

"It *is* a bedroom." He tried to act nonchalant about it, tugging her forward, toward the double doors that led into the hallway.

"*Your* bedroom?" She tugged back, slowing them down.

Which felt dangerous. And thrilling.

"Yes." *Gentleman's manners.* He swallowed hard.

As their eyes adjusted to the darkness, the only light ambient glow coming in from the terrace, she swept a slow gaze around the room.

The one room he'd made his own. From the marble fireplace to the sitting room's wingchairs and chess table. Including the carved wood four-poster bed, which is where her attention had paused.

The scrutiny edged into stark intimacy. An exposure of himself.

But it also seemed innocent.

A simple wanting to know more about him. Where he dreamt, tucked in, safe in the darkest hours.

She turned a little, until her gaze landed on the decorated dark tree, in the corner between the fireplace and the farthest window.

"What are those ribbons?" She began to walk forward.

But he held fast, their clasped hands tugging her to a stop.

With a gentle tug, he led her toward the light switches. Flicked on the one that lit up the lights on the tree.

"They're New Year's resolutions."

"All of them?"

"Yeah." All the ones on the trees in the main house? Maurice's creations. The ones in the bedroom? His. Private. From the heart.

"Can I see them?"

"Nope." *Not yet.* "Not till we've—"

"—had a drink," she finished, laughter in her voice.

Then he led her toward the double doors. Leading them out of the danger of the bedroom.

Sensing they were much closer to finding their missing bliss.

SEVEN

BEING SERVED hot chocolate in a giant red mug, on the fifth black leather barstool at a large island, in a gourmet kitchen torn straight from Architectural Digest—swaths of black granite counters flecked with shimmering turquoise, luxurious warm mahogany cabinetry, and an impressive stainless Viking range with dual ovens, six burners, and a griddle—Dali felt like a little kid.

But in an amazing grownup kinda way.

The kind where a dashing Logan—a man cast straight from her wildest fantasies—stared at her as if she'd become the only thing that interested him. In the entire world.

In the last fifteen minutes, he'd gone from undone bowtie tuxedo rebel to all-out alpha male—when he'd cut the catering staff loose, clearing them out of the kitchen in under five minutes, getting them to clean every surface on the way out—then had settled back into laidback sensitive gentleman.

A gentleman who had folded his tuxedo jacket over the back of the middle barstool, rolled up his shirtsleeves, then whipped them up some hot chocolate, like he'd been born in a kitchen. With *real* chocolate, bittersweet Valrhona that he'd chopped up into fine shards with a chef's knife. And whole milk. Couple teaspoons of sugar. A splash of vanilla. Plus a dollop of whipped cream at the end. Cream that he'd whisked into existence in a few minutes, while the chocolate melted and milk heated.

He'd turned off the kitchen lights, all except for the one over the range, which he'd dimmed.

Then he brought over the two prepared hot chocolates, in giant squat red mugs. She'd had to accept hers with two hands.

And they sat, huddled together, side by side on the two barstools at the end of the island. Near a dark-gray soapstone apron sink, below a large window that overlooked the terrace garden. With the tippy tops of a couple of lit evergreens peeking into view.

Lively music from the party drifted in, but it all fell into the background, feeling distant, far removed from the quieter party-for-two they'd claimed for themselves.

Logan stared at her over the rim of his mug—green eyes sparkling, with something close to mischief—as they lifted their hot chocolates for a first taste.

Decadent chocolatey goodness exploded over her tongue.

"Wow." She took another delicious hot sip, swirled it through her mouth, then swallowed. "You're like a hot chocolate ninja."

He tilted his head in a slight bow. "Something I've perfected over the last year. My comfort beverage."

"Well, you nailed it. Definitely comforting."

Over the next silent seconds, he drank from his mug.

All the while, her curiosity kept growing.

She glanced at a large silvery watch on his wrist.

"Rolex?"

"Omega."

"Platinum?"

"Eighteen-karat gold." He tilted the silvery white dial. "Omega calls it 'Canopus Gold.' It's a Speedmaster Moonwatch."

Of course, it was. Sounded impressive. And überexpensive.

She noticed the time on the watch face: twenty till midnight. "Well, we doin' this?"

The corners of his lips twitched, as if he fought a smile. He ran a tongue across his upper teeth. With his mouth closed.

Which made her want to kiss him, for some inexplicable reason.

He slid a hand into hers. "The sharing thing?"

"Yeah." The warm strength of his hand, the intimacy of his touch, did funny things to her. Made her feel safe. She hoped she could trust in that. Trust him.

"I'll share if you do."

"Deal." But to be absolutely sure, she narrowed her eyes at him. "No repercussions."

"No repercussions."

"Promise? No matter how bad?" Really bad.

"I promise."

"Even if criminal?"

His eyes widened a fraction. Then he leaned closer, murmuring conspiratorially, "*Especially* if something *you've* done is criminal." Doubt weighted his tone. His expression, dubious.

Just wait. "Okay. Here goes. You didn't invite me to your party."

He arched his brows a fraction. "This, I know."

"Or Cora."

He tipped a nod toward her. "Also something I know."

"We *stole* the invitation."

He nodded. "Because you figured you had to provide it to security at the door."

Which they had. "Annnd…"

She dragged out a lengthy pause, tension mounting in the silence.

He lowered his mug, resting it on the black granite countertop. A sign of his full undivided attention.

"I borrowed this dress."

His amused gaze darted back and forth, as if ferreting out some invisible secret flying around them.

"And shoes."

"Naturally."

"*Without* the owner's awareness."

"Ahhh…" He gave a single nod. "*Now* we're getting somewhere."

"All Cora's scheme."

"Sure."

"Still don't care?"

The interest in his eyes intensified. "Oh, I care."

"But… no repercussions?"

"Nope. You're off scot-free tonight."

"Okay." She blew out a relieved breath, then took another sip of hot chocolate. "Good."

"So why the stolen invitation and gown? Why all the subterfuge?"

"*Borrowed* gown and shoes. Going back into the fairy godmother's closet. After our limo-coach pops back into a pumpkin after midnight."

He angled a nod. "Duly noted. And not at midnight. Not tonight. I've got you until one."

Her brain snagged on that *I've got you* part. "You do?"

"Yep. You showed up late. And the party ends at one."

"Okay."

"So you were about to explain. Before the clarification diversion."

"Right." The man seemed determined to figure her out. And with every minute that ticked by as she got to know him, she wanted to share just a little bit more. "Cora wanted to bag a billionaire."

"One of the 'sharks'?" Amusement danced in his eyes as he quoted her term.

"Yeah."

"Well, don't tell Cora…" He leaned even closer, till their lips were only a few inches apart. "None of those sharks are billionaires. The only billionaire in the house is me." His tone deadened on the last part.

"Oh." And that billionaire had been drawn to Dali, not Cora.

Somehow, that seemed okay. Meant to be, even.

"They're all trust-fund kids. Set to inherit their wealth many decades from now. When they're old and gray."

"And you?"

He eased back. Far enough that cool air rushed in between them.

But he still held her hand.

Then he cleared his throat. "I inherited mine early."

A deep heaviness weighted his tone. Riddled with unspoken pain.

Dali tightened her grip, heart aching for him.

"It's okay for you to share. You're safe with me. No repercussions."

The least she could do.

Yet part of her wished she could offer more.

EIGHT

LOGAN STARED into Dali's beautiful black trusting eyes.

An incredible caring woman, one he hadn't expected.

Who gently urged him on, wanted him to feel safe.

Someone he'd desperately needed, long before he'd met her.

A woman he wanted as soon as he spotted her. While she'd discovered a moment of bliss in his New Year's winter garden. At the exact same time he had escaped and fled there as well.

They'd found each other. In a bizarre twist of fate.

He didn't give a damn about her crashing the party. Or that she'd "borrowed" her outfit.

Because fate had played a hand in bringing both of them together.

And he felt like the luckiest man on the planet.

She'd finally trusted him with what plagued her. Had taken that chance.

Then she had urged him to do the same.

They sat close to one another, holding hands, in the dim light of his kitchen.

Warmth from the caterer's baking and his hot-chocolate making still radiated into the space.

The DJ's music, from several rooms down, faded into the distant background. Drowned out by the hammering pulse against his eardrum.

He licked his lips, tasting the rich chocolate and sweetness from the cream.

She rubbed a gentle thumb over the back of his hand, searching his eyes.

And as they sat there, over comforting mugs of hot chocolate, he decided to go for it.

"This is my childhood home. We spent summers here. Most weekends over winters. Every holiday. This kitchen is where Mom taught me to make hot chocolate, and bake all kinds of things. Dad roasted turkeys over there"—he nodded toward the oven—"every Thanksgiving. My younger brother, Dillon, sat at the barstool behind me, icing dozens of gingerbread cookies at Christmastime."

Her face brightened as he spoke.

"Sounds wonderful."

"It was." He let out a heavy sigh. "Dali, why don't you drink?"

She glanced down at her mug, then his, then back up to meet his gaze. "I don't like it. Hate being impaired. Even a little."

"Me too. But only since earlier this year. Because my entire family, Dad, Mom, and Dillon, were all killed in a helicopter crash.

Her eyes widened. Her hand tightened around his. "Oh, wow. Logan, I'm so sorry."

"Thanks." But that hadn't been the worst of it. "Dad had been drinking. Then he got behind the stick and piloted that night. They'd been visiting friends in the next town over.

"I was supposed to go with them. But I'd gotten into a fight with Dad and he'd told me to stay behind."

Tears sparkled in her eyes. "And you never saw them again."

"Never heard from them again." He pinched his eyes shut, a cramp forming in his throat.

Still clasping his hand, she shifted, coming closer.

Softness pressed to his eyelids. *Her lips.* Gentle kisses.

"You survived, Logan. You were meant to be here," she murmured.

He drew in a deep breath, then opened his eyes. Stared into hers.

"With you." The only thing holding him together at that moment.

"With me."

A wobbly smile curved over her lips. "*Now* can I see those New Year's resolutions?"

He glanced at his watch. Eight minutes till midnight. "Yes."

They left their half-empty mugs on the island and his coat on the barstool.

Hand in hand, they walked down the dimly lit corridor.

Soft clicks of their heels on the marble floor echoed off the plastered walls.

A tension vibrated in the silence between them.

Not uncomfortable. Just... deeper.

Like they'd grown closer with their confessions.

And he wanted to learn even more about her.

"What do you do, Dali?"

"Attending university." She glanced up at him. "Months away from my law degree."

No wonder she'd been so worried about her criminal activities.

"What kind of law?"

"Environmental." Passion colored her tone.

"Nice. A field close to my heart."

"Really? What do you do?"

"Real estate development. With a goal of wilderness preservation," he was quick to add.

They stepped back into the darkness of his bedroom. White lights twinkled on the tree in the corner. Ambient light glowed in from the terrace garden, but he left the hall doors halfway open. Ever the gentleman.

Taking care, so neither of them tripped on the sheepskin rug near the side of the bed, he led her wide and around, along the windows, then up to the tree.

"The ones on this tree are *my* New Year's resolutions."

She scanned over the tree. "There's a lot of them."

"I need a lot of resolutions."

A few dozen.

And with her, several more.

"Take a couple of them."

A half-smile formed. "For me?"

"If you'd like."

Her fingertips hovered over the silk ivory ribbons. She lifted one from the upper right. Then took a second from the middle, in front of her.

"You too."

"Okay." He chose his at random, one from up high, another that dangled in front of her nose.

She gave his hand a light squeeze. "Before we read them, could we add one?"

He turned toward her. "I was going to ask the same thing. What's yours?"

"If we don't have any other plans, we meet in your garden, next year at New Year's."

"That's what I was going to say. Only it's *our* garden. And we should *make* those plans."

"As a *joint* resolution?"

"Yeah." He loved the sound of that. Their garden. Solid plans. Joint. With her.

"Wearing that gown."

She laughed. "You *want* me to steal it?"

"It's beautiful on you."

She pulled wide some of the skirt's purple-green layers and glanced down. "Doesn't make me look a mermaid goddess?"

"Mermaid...?" He frowned, not following. At all.

"Nothing. Something silly Cora said."

"If anything..." He tucked a rogue spiral of dark hair behind her ear, staring down into her black eyes. "You are an enchanting garden nymph. One-of-a-kind. Stunning."

"Oh, wow." Her eyes widened. "I love your vision."

As do I.

In a sudden rush, the noise and excitement from the party amplified.

The final countdown to the new year had begun.

He blew out a steadying breath. Feeling as if he stood on the precipice. Of an adventure. "Will you read your resolutions first?"

She gave a nod, then angled her first ribbon toward the light. "Be honest. Take a chance."

Her face lit up with warmth at her resolutions. "I was. And I am."

When she tipped a nod toward him, he read his. "Be brave. Change your life."

He smiled. "I am. And I have. Starting with you."

Because of you.

They eased together, wrapping their arms around each other.

Distant echoes of the shouted countdown filtered in from the hall.

"Want to commit to our joint resolution?" Yeah. He went there.

"Commit." She stared up into his eyes. "*Our* garden. Next year at New Year's?"

Ten...

"Yes." Definite. What he wanted. Without doubt. "And every moment till then." Everything. All or nothing. Life and time were too precious to waste.

Seven...

"Yes, Logan. I want to commit. To all of it."

Five...

He leaned down. "To spending a brand-new year."

Three...

"With you," she murmured.

One...

They touched noses, brushed lips. Then they deepened the kiss, holding on tight, surrendering to the passion igniting between them.

Long seconds later, they eased back, but stayed locked in their tight embrace.

"Happy New Year." Murmured together.

Joyful wonder widened her eyes.

Eternal gratitude warmed his heart.

That he'd discovered an incredible partner. That they had daring plans.

And that he'd found hope.

EPILOGUE

THE FOLLOWING YEAR, Dali and Logan wandered onto the garden terrace, on New Year's Eve, as they'd agreed.

A garden refreshed for the occasion, bursting with twice as much white-lit foliage.

Scented by fragrant blooms of rose and wisteria.

And that glorious sweetness of cool mountain air.

Only the second time around, they rendezvoused a little earlier.

Just before sunset. Under a big blue sky.

Because the view from the terrace during the daytime? Spectacular.

Their palatial house overlooked three mountain peaks, covered in pine forest frosted with a few inches of overnight snow.

Yet on that day, instead of a wrought iron bistro hovering near the edge by the railing, a brilliant white arbor arched. Dripping with evergreen boughs, white rose blossoms, and a pale purple haze of wisteria.

And rather than being alone on the terrace, friends had gathered to join them.

For their wedding.

Cora stood off to the left, as her maid of honor, in *her own* draping off-the-shoulder gown of pale violet. Beside three of Dali's university friends as bridesmaids.

Logan faced Dali, wearing an expression of stark gratitude. Handsome as ever, in his same bespoke black tuxedo, all tall, dark, and broad. Breathtaking.

Thomas, Luke, Bryan and Coby lined up as groomsman, in solid support of their lifelong friend. All wore pale violet cummerbunds to match the bridesmaids.

She had graduated that May.

Then Logan had hired her. To ensure his company acted in harmony with the natural lands and wildlife around all their developments. And to set an example for other developers.

Cora waved at Luke. The besotted man gave her a lopsided smile in return. They'd begun dating a few months back. After Cora had strung along all four sharks. While she tried to decide which one to settle on.

In the end, love upended whatever scheme Cora played.

Exactly as matters of the heart should go.

Only their friends had been invited to witness the small private ceremony. With Thomas—the best man and new online-ordained minister—planning to step forward at Logan's cue and officiate their ceremony.

Because the larger celebration would take place at the party, later that night.

At which, they planned to stay for only the first hour.

Before they jetted off for two weeks of sunny bliss, to

some secluded tropical isle that Logan had kept secret from her.

Logan let out a deep sigh, pure joy in his expression, as he stepped toward her.

"You are stunning," he murmured, taking her hands in his.

"Not your garden nymph." No violet-green gown. She and Cora had returned the gowns. Silent about what they'd done. And the wealthy woman who owned them had been none the wiser.

"*Always* my garden nymph." He swept a gaze down her gown. "Yet in that gown? Dazzling."

He'd spared no expense for her dream gown. But in the end, she'd insisted on a local seamstress.

Who'd designed a classic beautiful wedding gown, specially made for her.

The simple white satin strapless gown flowed naturally, as if an extension of her body. Adorned with delicate botanical embroidery and a touch of sequins, gracing the curve above her right breast, embellishing the flare of her left hip, then undulating above the hem and border of the gown's small train.

And tucked through a few sweeping curls at her crown —above sleeked tresses that cascaded down her back— rested an elegant diamond tiara.

A gift he'd given her.

Something borrowed. And treasured.

Because his mom had worn the tiara when she'd married his dad.

"Thank you. For everything."

He stared deep into her eyes. "All for you."

Something he'd said more than once. Mostly regarding his heart.

Sometimes about his wealth.

Because the billions he had? Only meant something if they could be funneled for good.

"Not why I'm marrying you."

Logan could be dirt poor, and she'd still want him.

Because she'd fallen in love with the man who'd wanted to ease her worry on a New Year's Eve. After he'd suffered for nearly a year with an unimaginable loss of his own. The man who wanted to right the world every day. For her and for everyone else. In any way he could.

Mirth sparkled in his vivid green eyes. "It's because I whip up a mean hot chocolate."

"Totally." No lie there. "And because you have the most amazing resolutions."

"The best ones?" He searched her eyes. "Being brave. Changing our lives."

"Taking a chance," she added. "And being honest." With themselves and one another.

"And the most important of all..." He gave her hands a light squeeze.

They stared into each other's eyes, spoke their favorite resolution, from their hearts, as a shared vow...

"Committing to you."

❄

Thank You!

Thank you for experiencing all the delightful mistletoe mischief in *Half-baked Holidays: A Romantic Comedy Holiday Collection*.

If you enjoyed the stories, please express your love for the collection by recommending it to friends in person, by email, on Goodreads, and through book clubs and reader groups.

And if you value reviews to help guide you into your next books, as we do, please help other readers by sharing your review on your favorite retailer and book community sites.

❄

Incredible thanks to everyone for extending your love of *Half-baked Holidays: A Romantic Comedy Holiday Collection*.

Reviews are cherished love notes to authors
and tantalizing invitations to readers.
Appreciated by all.

Want to Read More?

Dive into the romance of the
No Weddings series...
No Weddings
One Funeral
Two Bar Mitzvahs
Three Christmases
For Valentine's

The first four novels can be found in...
No Weddings Limited Edition Box Set: Books 1-4

Read more of your favorite characters from the No
Weddings series in the spinoff
Unbreakable Series...

Kiki & Darren's romance ignites in...
Heartbreaker

Mase & Leilani's passion flares in...
Rule Breaker

Ben & Shay flirt with danger in...
Lawbreaker

Want to Read EVEN More?

Icebreaker **and** ***Ball Breaker***
AND
**a brand-new contemporary romance series
are all coming soon!**

Be the first to receive preorder alerts, exclusive bonus gifts,
and occasional free stories...

Join our Bastion Family Adventurers!
https://www.katbastion.com/email-subscription/

Escape into award-winning time travel romance in the
novels of the **Highland Legends** series...
Forged in Dreams and Magick
Bound by Wish and Mistletoe
Born of Mist and Legend
Found in Flame and Moonlight

Adventure in a paranormal short-story
series, a spinoff of the Highland Legends series
THE TRAVELER: Initiate Years ...
Veil of Realms
Secrets of Alexandria
Panther Rising
Stones of Power
Highland Magick

ALSO BY KAT & STONE BASTION

No Weddings Series

No Weddings · One Funeral

Two Bar Mitzvahs · Three Christmases

For Valentine's

Unbreakable Series

Heartbreaker · Rule Breaker · Lawbreaker

Forthcoming: *Ball Breaker · Icebreaker*

Comic Book Date Series

The Accidental May the 4th Comic Book Date

The Unbelievable Made on a Dare Comic Book Date

The Irresistible 4th of July Comic Book Date

Standalone Novels & Novelettes

Brand New Year · The Espionage Effect

Highland Legends Series

Forged in Dreams and Magick · Bound by Wish and Mistletoe

Born of Mist and Legend · Found in Flame and Moonlight

THE TRAVELER: Initiate Years

Veil of Realms · Secrets of Alexandria · Panther Rising

Stones of Power · Highland Magick

Romantic Poetry for Charity

Utterly Loved

Heartbreaker

Kiki...

For a blessed few hours, I forgot.

Loading Zone did that to me. The nightclub's Industrial Grunge feel, which I'd helped design with its exposed brick and rusted steel, wrapped itself around me like a comfortable blanket. Heavy bass thumped, vibrating into my bones. My thighs burned from dancing back-to-back songs. Three lemon drop martinis in the last two hours hummed warmth through my veins.

"C'mon," my sister Kendall shouted above the loud music as she grasped my hand, then tugged me forward. "My toes are numb."

Out of breath, I nodded and we headed toward the corner booth the eight of us had crammed into earlier. I dance-walked in the narrow path through the crowd behind her, each step a hip shake and head toss to the pulsing rhythm.

The moment we reached the table, our oldest sister, Kristen, pulled her husband from the booth. "Time for us to go. Jason has an early flight tomorrow."

Cade, our brother and silent partner of Loading Zone, guided his new wife, Hannah, out right after them. "Last dance, Mrs. Michaelson?"

Which left Cade's two best friends: the scruffy prodigy surfer Mase, his former roommate; and clean-cut businessman Ben, the other owner of Loading Zone. I slid over the black distressed leather before landing in the center of the wide, shallow booth to face the dance floor while Mase abandoned his spot on the opposite side to anchor the end next to me.

I grasped the stem of my martini glass, sipped the last bit of the tart lemon drop, then let out a happy-buzz sigh. Being around these three—including rising-star architect Kendall—all of them with their shit together, lent some grounding *yin* to my artistic *yang*.

"Sex on a stick, twelve o'clock," Kendall announced.

My heart suddenly slammed into my ribs. But I exhaled slowly, trying to hide my reaction.

I'd been excited about tonight for several reasons: banish my secret problems from my head, surround myself with my favorite peeps, and *Darren Cole*.

Ben snorted out laughter while Mase dropped me a deadpan look. "'Sex on a *stick*'?"

I shot Mase a sidelong glare and elbowed him in the ribs.

He grunted and nudged my arm away.

By the time I glanced up, corded forearms shot over the outer edge of the table. Large hands planted with a hard smack on the brushed metal tabletop. A familiar folded strip of paper skittered out from his fingers, sliding in a wide arc toward Ben.

My breath caught as I stared into Darren's dark green eyes. A lock of his shaggy black hair fell over his forehead as he tilted his face downward. He set his jaw, expression hardening, as a scuffle between four guys unfolded right behind him, the apparent cause of his sudden hand-plant. He gave me a piercing look. "Twenty minutes."

Then he turned and grasped the nearest offender by the scruff of his shirt. Security arrived an instant later and manhandled the others into submission.

As Darren flexed his left arm while leading his guy toward the exit of the club, the tapered point of a tribal tattoo peeked out from the back collar of Darren's black T-shirt. My imagination began to paint what lay hidden from view: thick black ink arcing across sculpted back muscles, a woven design that twisted downward toward his tight...

"What's that?" Kendall leaned over the table.

I tore my gaze away from Darren and reached for the note, but Kendall snatched up the slip of paper first. She unfolded it and read its message aloud, "'*Gimme a ride? K.*'"

"Oh, sure." Mase took a long pull from his beer, then swallowed. "Kendall gets to innuendo the fuck out of this, but I don't?"

Ben arched a brow. "Twenty minutes. That's one helluva ride."

"Shut up. Both of you. Guys objectify women. We can do the same. And it's a ride home, smartass." I tried to shoot Ben an annoyed glare, but the corners of my mouth twitched into a smile and ruined the whole thing.

"*Suuure*...a ride home." Mase winked at me, then glanced over to where Darren strode along the edge of the room as he headed back toward his DJ booth. "I suppose he qualifies."

"Worthy of objectifying? Darren more than qualifies." I pinched the message *meant for Darren's eyes only* and ripped it from Kendall's grasp. "He doesn't say much," I continued. "Leaves the club with different women. Built like the perfect male specimen..."

Ben choked on his beer. "And what are we? Male rejects?"

"Ewww." Kendall scowled. "That's incestuous."

"You're like our brothers. Can't even..." I scrunched my

nose and blanked out my mind, willing myself not to visualize it.

"Not looking for love?" Ben asked, tone softening.

At that, all of our gazes drifted toward the dance floor. One of the last songs of the night streamed a fast tempo from the speakers, but in the center of a thinning crowd, Cade and Hannah stood oblivious. Wrapped together, they swayed to a slow rhythm only they seemed to hear. The look of adoration on their faces as they stared deep into each other's eyes spoke volumes.

"No," I said with absolute conviction. "Heartache lies down that road."

Mase laid a gentle hand on mine. "As your pseudo-brother, I'm warning you: Be careful."

I had no idea whether he meant Darren specifically or men in general. It didn't really matter. I'd learned my love lesson early. And I'd never trusted a guy enough to let one hurt me since.

Darren? The only kind of guy I was willing to play with. A beautiful man I refused to form any attachment to— easy to leave.

The quintessential heartbreaker.

In Darren's truck. Again. A vast awkward distance between us. *Again.*

The drive took only about ten minutes. But the ride home from Loading Zone in Philly's Old City Arts District to the outskirts of sleepy Glenhaven—the third since last summer—stretched eternal.

Why? A hookup shouldn't be this difficult.

My gaze shifted toward him. Powerful hands gripped

the steering wheel, thumbs knocking some unheard drumbeat into the silence of the cab. Sculpted forearms stretched up toward cut biceps that vanished under the thin black fabric of the T-shirt that hugged them. His expression was serious, but relaxed. As if he didn't feel the weight of the moment like I did.

Now or never, Kiki.

I took a deep breath and ran a flattened hand over the gauzy material of my skirt, trying to calm myself. Then I inched closer to him, needing some sort of validation that whatever tenuous thing we had between us was moving toward something...fun...instead of away from it.

Tonight didn't have to be a big deal. He either wanted me or didn't. Two other platonic drop-offs didn't mean anything significant. Maybe he was shy. Or a gentleman.

As we drove, yellow pools of light from wrought iron lampposts marked the passing time in a visual cadence. *Light...dark. Light...dark.* The streetlights soon began to feel like a countdown, as if they mocked me for just sitting passively in their spotlights.

Yet how to breach the uncomfortable silence? My mind tumbled over the possibilities: *How did your sound board glide tonight? Wow, how 'bout the heavy bass on that last song?*

He cleared his throat, beating me to it. "Sooo...talk to me. How's the art going?"

"Good." *Good? Really?* I winced at my pathetic attempt at conversation.

We made the second-to-last turn, my time running out, as he gave a single nod in reply.

Buck up, Kiki. You either want him or you don't. Stop being a pussy. "Actually, it's a smaller sculpture. A single orchid sprouting from a rocky riverbed."

He glanced my way. "You work with metal, right?"

"Yeah." I leaned back, staring out the windshield, finally calming a bit as I thought about my art. "This piece is bronze. The lone color is the violet on the flower."

"Sounds cool." His voice lowered. He cleared his throat again.

Had he moved closer?

Impossible. He was driving. Behind the steering wheel, as always.

Yet our legs nearly touched. The rough denim, tight over his thigh, had slid over the tan leather seat to within an inch of my bared knee; he'd spread his legs wider.

The man already consumed most of the space in the truck with his commanding presence. But instead of moving away, I automatically drew closer. My thundering pulse throbbed heavier, warmer...lower.

I swallowed hard, attempting to find my way back to the conversation. "How did your night go?" Maybe his sound board was a medium for his art, like metal was for me.

"Good." The corner of his mouth twitched into a barely perceptible grin, then relaxed.

He dropped his right hand from the steering wheel and floated it in the infinitesimal space between us. Gentle pressure rubbed through the flimsy fabric that covered my upper thigh.

My gaze lowered from the dashboard at the exact moment the knuckle of his index finger trailed in slow motion up the skin under my hem.

I held my breath.

I haven't been imagining things.

But then his hand suddenly lifted and fisted. His expression hardened as he stared straight ahead. We made the final turn onto my street, and he eased off the gas, letting us coast. The ride I'd been waiting all night for—six long months and two failed attempts for—appeared to be over.

We rolled to a stop in front of the white picket fence that surrounded the darling butter-yellow Victorian. Then he shifted the truck into park, letting it idle.

Refusing to give up, especially when I sensed him struggling with an attraction we both knew was real, I made a final direct attempt. "You don't have to drive right off. You could come in for a drink."

"No, I can't."

"Why not?" The two words tripped out flippant in my pitiful effort to sound nonchalant.

"You're Cade's little sister."

"No, I'm n—" I blinked.

The pad of his finger pressed to my lips. Warm. Firm. Suddenly, I thought of nothing else. My whole world became our tantalizing first contact.

He didn't move. Simply stared at me.

I closed my eyes. My head eased back against the headrest, but the contact remained as my lips pursed into the gentlest kiss against his fingertip. I wanted to flick my tongue out, taste him. But then he pulled away.

I blinked my eyes open.

He'd half-twisted on the seat toward me. "You deserve better than a one-night fuck, Kiki."

"What I deserve," I muttered, then snorted.

Damn right, I deserve better than that.

But one night was all I could handle.

"Doesn't matter." What I continued to tell myself. "What I want right now is you." There, I'd said it. Out in the open. Bold and direct.

"What you deserve *does* matter. Don't ever forget it." His voice hardened with every word. His dark brows furrowed to the point a deep crease marred the tanned skin between them.

Without thinking, I reached up and pressed my thumb along that vertical line, massaging until his face began to relax.

He stared at me with renewed intensity. "What are you doing?"

"Trying to get you to chill out." I let my thumb slide a fraction to the right until I found a pressure point, then I spread the rest of my fingertips across the line of his eyebrow. "Is it working?"

"No." The corners of his mouth twitched again.

"Liar."

"Okay. A little."

"Seriously, though," I continued as if I hadn't been distracted by his impressive scowl. "I'm an excellent one-night fuck."

He jerked his head away, then lapsed into a coughing fit.

I arched a brow. "What? Don't think so?"

He shook his head. "No." His mouth fell open. "I mean, I'm sure you are." He blew out a heavy sigh, cheeks puffing from the effort. "You just..."

"Unnerve you?"

"Yes." He thrust a splayed hand into the open air between us with the curt word. "Are you trying to kill me?"

A smile began to curve my lips. "No, I'm just trying to—"

"Don't say it."

The word hung on the tip of my tongue. "You know I'm thinking it."

"Stop thinking it." He took a measured breath, his chest gradually rising, then falling.

Enjoying the loaded tension between us, I remained still, waiting.

When he turned toward me again, I leaned closer and deeply inhaled his earthy scent. "Look. This doesn't have to be complicated just because I'm Cade's sister. You're an adult. I'm an adult. Aren't you attracted to me?"

Every telltale sign he'd shown suggested that he wanted me. But I'd never encountered so much resistance in a guy before. Then again, I'd never had one in my sights so long before either. I ignored the implications in that.

"Of course I am." He draped an arm along the top of the seatback.

His warmth lured me in, and I edged even closer until my entire side crushed against his. He made no move to stop me and didn't flinch away, but his lengthy pause indicated that he resisted committing to anything.

"All it has to be is one night," I whispered, my lips nearly touching the warm skin of his neck.

Another heavy sigh ruffled the hair above my ear, shooting chill bumps down my side. "You gotta know, if I could...I would. It *is* complicated. I can't explain. But no matter how badly either of us want to, this can't happen."

I blinked, confused and lost in uncharted territory. Never had a guy not taken the bait I'd offered. And he was being so nice about it. My mind couldn't process what was happening. "You want me."

"Fuck, yes. I mean, no." He growled in frustration. "Goddammit, Kiki. Just get out of the truck. Please."

I pulled away from him and straightened in my seat, almost laughing at the desperation in his tone. Then I dared a glance at him. His expression grew tortured. A tiny part of me felt bad for putting him in a position I didn't understand. The rest of me beamed that I wasn't the only sexually frustrated one in the vehicle.

Not yet willing to admit defeat, I gave him a smile and grasped the cold metal door handle. "Thanks for the ride, Darren."

I wouldn't ask for one again. But I didn't need to. The seeds had been planted. My work was done. Either he wanted me enough to get past whatever obstacle was cock-blocking his way, or he didn't.

Meanwhile, I'd go back to the life I'd been trying to forget, once my mind-numbing buzz wore off.

I wanted to glance over my shoulder as I unfastened the painted wooden gate, double-check to see if he was still watching, but I fought the urge.

The low hum of his idling truck engine remained unchanged. But had his mind?

This lonely girl can only hope.

Enjoy the rest of the romance...
Heartbreaker

Found in Flame and Moonlight

Eight minutes was all Chelsea Smith had. All she needed. *Hopefully*.

The heavy wooden door to Professor MacLaren's private office snicked closed behind her. With a subtle suggestion from her mind, the tumblers reengaged within its lock, a deadbolt she'd "picked" with similar mental ease mere seconds ago.

On her next inhale of cooler undisturbed air, the distinctive scents of age washed over her: that certain spice of centuries-old leather, a mustiness of layered dust, the sweetness of yellowing paper in a prized collection of ancient books.

The room's furnishings echoed its owner's passion for antiquities. Within a sizable entry, a vintage coffee-colored Chesterfield sofa with matching wingchairs hovered at the edge of a burgundy-and-gold Aubusson carpet. Along the side and far wall, relics from exotic locales perched from various niches between precisely stacked scholarly tomes in massive bookcases. And beyond a sizable polished wood desk and its stately leather chair, within tall display cases that flanked a large window, treasured discoveries from historic digs rested on glass shelves.

Yet one particular artifact stood apart from the rest. The sole reason for her break-in. And the item occupied the nearest corner of his polished wood desk, exposed. No bookcase niche. No protective case.

"Such unfathomable *power*," Chelsea murmured

toward the rectangular object, at once fascinated and intrigued. More than she'd been about anything in her first twenty-two years of an immortal life hiding-in-plain sight among "normal" humans.

Her excitement even eclipsed what she'd witnessed from the other side of that window while walking to MacLaren's lecture less than an hour ago.

Though her mind still reeled about that discovery as well.

Because something very *not human* had stood near that power-drenched box, partially transparent, as if not fully materialized into the human world. And that shirtless muscular something had resembled artistic depictions of male angelic warriors, only skewed darker and more sinister with its dusky olive skin, inky black wings, and blue-green prismatic eyes.

And the enigmatic creature had stared directly at her, eyes narrowing, puzzlement twisting his sharp features as Chelsea blatantly stared back. He'd seemed surprised. That she could detect him? Or perhaps that their paths had intersected in the first place.

Yet inside the professor's locked office, no sign of the dark angel remained.

Seven minutes.

The forceful vibration of the artifact's unique power was what had caught her attention from the other side of the window. It had radiated an exhilarating and complex energy, beckoning her like a siren's call.

"Invitation accepted," she whispered.

With slow breaths, Chelsea banked her excitement. Not hard to achieve. Her kind, further evolved humans, born-and-bred assassins, had been trained through millennia to suppress emotion.

"Yeah." She let out a soft snort. "Look how well *that* turned out."

Members of her race had recently evolved again. And an underground faction had organically formed. One that no longer sought to squelch their emotions. That strong minority yearned for something greater, a deeper meaning to their eternal life.

Months ago, Chelsea had been secretly contacted by them. The founders had detected her tendency to operate on the fringe of acceptability. Of course, she'd joined their cause without hesitation.

In the hours and days following that pivotal decision, she'd eased the cognitive restraints that had hobbled her. They had warned her that she would suffer unimaginable internal struggle. Yet nothing had prepared her for the cascade of emotions. One in particular had caused an enormous dissonance with her inherited vocation.

Empathy had bled into her black-and-white world.

An *assassin's* world.

And that problematic emotion had caused a thunderstorm of chaotic gray.

Six minutes.

Focus, Chelsea. She took measured steps toward the charged artifact, noting its unusual features. A foot long, half that wide and tall, a rectangular box sat encased in layers of elaborate metallic latticework. The gleaming designs that adorned its corners and edges were comprised of various metals from differing artistry. But beneath those ornate motifs, simpler flat sides were fashioned from a beautiful bluish-silver metal with a slight sparkle to its sheen.

Indirect bright light glowed in from the large window, but as Chelsea approached, an aura of energy haloed around the box. Infinitesimal particles glittered beyond its

surfaces, flashes of silver and gold visible to her preternat-
ural eyes.

Five minutes.

Which meant MacLaren's lecture in his beloved
Advanced Theories in Archaeology had concluded. Earlier,
Chelsea had obediently endured the graduate-level course
with fifteen other classmates until she'd politely excused
herself at the last and most opportune moment. A correct
amount of respectful time from a valued student. The
perfect window of plausible deniability should her burglary
plans go awry.

Students typically waylaid him after his lectures, but to
be certain, she extended her superhuman hearing. Down a
wide sidewalk between buildings, across a grassy quad, and
into the cozy window-lined room that the tenured professor
claimed as his own, she detected the voices of eager students
who had indeed detained him. Which enabled him to wax
eloquent about the week's series and his latest obsession:
prehistoric artifacts handed down by gods, breadcrumbs to
the secrets of mysterious civilizations.

"But you've been keeping the biggest secret of all right
here in your office, haven't you?" Chelsea murmured as she
paused within reach of the object.

Four minutes.

Plenty of time to abort, to walk away without detection.

"I don't *need* to be here." Sound reason.

And yet, need had become relative.

For in the months following her recent evolution, an
undefinable hunger had begun to grow that nothing satisfied. A craving for a deeper purpose. Not the deadly one
mandated by her ancestry. Not even the glimmer of hope
that her emerging faction offered.

"Something personal," she murmured, staring at the

box. She'd been hunting a cause that matched her sudden passion for life. Unique and special. Sparked by her newfound awakening. "Worthy. And all my own."

Because every action she'd taken in life, from actual missions to basic periphery cover, had been by her race's directive. Even attending university. Particularly MacLaren's courses.

But for the first time, she operated on her own volition. Because before that morning, she hadn't been privy to any details of *why* MacLaren had become a person of interest. Until one shining detail had made itself known, flashing its undeniable energy straight toward her.

Therefore, the risk of exposure? While investigating an object as exceptional as what she hoped to discover about herself?

More than acceptable.

While she continued to listen, the distinct voices of six fellow grad students dwindled to two hardcore disciples. They peppered the professor with questions, theories, and offers of assistance on his next expedition. Groveling, as usual. But MacLaren had their number. And only a couple of minutes remained of his scheduled patience.

Chelsea drew a deep breath to calm her riotous—clearly *not* suppressed—emotions.

Instinct screamed the intricate box held her destiny. Even if she had no idea why.

But as she took a final step and reached out a hand to touch, its unique power reacted to her proximity with accelerating vibrations of energy—plenty of evidence to back up that gut feeling.

Three minutes.

MacLaren shooed out his fan club with his parting excuses and locked up the classroom.

Right as Chelsea hovered a hand over the artifact.

Energy emanated upward from that bluish-silver top, charging the air with electrons that sizzled and sparked. Warmth bathed her palm. Friendly. Inviting. *Intoxicating.*

Until a sense of grave danger spiked in those scant inches between the mysterious metal and her skin. And an unfamiliar feeling of trepidation tripped down her spine. Like some cosmic warning.

Chelsea paused, then blinked heavily, thrown by the sudden unfriendliness of the box and her own emotion about it. She wiggled her fingers within the box's charged aura and considered her impulsive actions. And their unknown ramifications. With the artifact. And MacLaren.

An extensive list of potentialities scrolled through her advanced mind. But the calculations magnified when she removed the laws of the known universe and input alternate realities. Involving energized boxes. And dark angels. And supposedly regular professors that capture the attention of a race of assassins.

Ninety seconds.

"So many possibilities," she murmured about the upside. *Too many variables to calculate.*

Chelsea snorted and shook her head with a slight smile. "I've never been afraid of anything in my life." Headlong into the adventure. The only way she saw the world.

The leather heels of MacLaren's loafers clicked down the nearest sidewalk.

Less than a minute. Before her trespass was discovered.

Urgency fired through her veins. She tensed her arm and lowered her hand, ready to touch no matter the outcome. To finally complete some circuit she'd begun to sense, as if the dark matter hovering between the spaces in the universe needed her help.

The charged air rippled with a stronger dose of caution. Chelsea narrowed her eyes at the box.

Are you trying to communicate with me?

That the inanimate object had sentience, as opposed to some other force out in the ether, gave her pause. Deadly animals and insects often displayed vivid warnings of their lethal venom.

But why lead me here with such clear invitation? Do you not want me to touch?

The warning vibration wavered back and forth in response as the additional questions crossed her mind. Not quite a yes, not quite a no. That it wanted her there, perhaps. But not to touch? *Orrr...*

"Not yet?" Barely an inch existed.

A hot glow sparkled into existence between her and the artifact, golden and shimmering. The box's energy extended an exquisite representation of agreement in its special language.

"Fascinating." Mesmerizing.

The artifact's seductive power continued to astound.

Have you taunted MacLaren with such scandalous invitation?

No sooner had she posed the mental question, than an answer rippled forth. Only that message vibrated not from the artifact, but from somewhere out in the ether. *No.* Crystal clear. Not as any legible word, but a negative in resonance.

The energized box did not wait on that desk for the professor.

At that moment, the artifact existed for a singular purpose: to join its immense power with hers.

MacLaren's footfalls began to click down the tiles of the building's corridor.

Energy spiked from the box again. Even while its power rippled another caution: *Not yet.* The message clearly vibrated from the object, not the ether.

But unraveling the mysteries of a higher consciousnesses in matter and space had to wait.

Adrenaline surged through her. "Out of time."

Golden sparks fountained up from its metallic top, singeing her palm. *Not yet!*

"When?" Chelsea choked out a laugh at the box. "*After* he has campus security cuff me?"

MacLaren's key slid into the lock.

Her pulse raced, the thump of her heart a drumbeat in her ears.

Now or never! she argued to the unseen gatekeepers.

Tiny clicks echoed as tumblers released in the lock's mechanism.

The door edge scraped over its frame, the only means of a clean escape swinging open and her window of opportunity closing right along with it.

Half-assed alibies spun through her mind, all utterly ridiculous: *I followed a burglar in, I needed to lie down and only your pin-tucked sofa would do, I saw a black-winged angel with sparkling blue-green eyes staring out your window.* Voicing that last factoid? Bordered on certifiable insanity.

But at the last split second between clean infiltration and utter discovery—right as her anxiety skyrocketed—a powerful vacuum slammed her hand down that remaining inch.

A scorching current charged up through her palm from the metal. Blinding power and incredible pleasure flashed through her being.

MacLaren's office vanished.

And a realm of absolute nothingness descended.

Gawain Brodie sucked in a stunned breath as the inside of his chest...*boomed.*

Thunder? Confused, he frowned but refused to break stride. He raced down an earthen footpath in the shadowy forest to rejoin his warriors; he'd been ambushed while scouting. And since no cloud marred the late-afternoon sky, he shook off the jarring sensation.

Faster! Scant seconds remained. Clan Brodie had been exposed. Their castle's centuries-old secret somehow breached.

Blood from three attackers speckled his arms and chest. Yet the last one's dying words bore evidence of the exposure: *Your magick castle is ours!*

A tang from the skirmish coated his tongue, pungent earth and the coppery taste of blood. Anger churned in his gut. Ferocity pumped through his veins. Single-minded determination overcame burning muscles as he sought to vanquish whatever enemy they faced.

Intent on cutting time, he broke into a sunny glade, ran across rippling purple blooms of heather, then rejoined the well-worn trail. Yet as he rounded the gnarled trunk of an ancient yew, a sudden awareness made him veer wide in the turn.

Alongside the path, lacy fronds of bracken trembled. Then a blur of motion burst forth.

Dark garb registered in his peripheral vision. As did the gleam of a swinging sword.

He unsheathed his own sword, then blocked a strike meant to cleave his neck.

Never pausing his momentum, Gawain twisted his body and shifted forward, swinging his weapon over. Then he tightened his blade down at the last moment for the killing blow.

To his surprise, the swords clashed. Punishing vibration jarred his bones from hand to arm, shoulder to neck, till they rattled a final quiver down through his teeth.

The attacker—a male with flaxen hair, of similar height and breadth to the threesome he'd more easily dispatched—merely sounded a low grunt.

With greater determination, Gawain thrust.

In equal measure, his opponent parried.

Fury darkened his attacker's eyes.

Exhilaration fired through Gawain's veins.

Their deadly battle-dance continued with strikes and blocks, thrusts and parries. Each next metallic crash rang out with echoing menace.

"At long last, a worthy opponent," Gawain murmured.

Gawain arced his sword back around, but once the tip swung skyward, he twisted, tucked, then thrust from a lower angle.

The soldier deflected then stepped aside, just as well trained, equally gifted.

"Aye. An 'opponent' who'll impale yer bloody arse like a stuck pig," the soldier replied in an English accent. A sick hunger gleamed in his eye.

Amused, Gawain relaxed his stance and drew back his weapon. He tilted his head and narrowed his eyes. "Why eat pig when you can dine like a king?"

The man's expression fell. As did the tip of his sword while he gave a heavy blink and furrowed his brow. "What're you on about?"

In the next heartbeat, Gawain lunged with incredible

speed. The tip of his sword led the way, piercing the man's heart before he was able to draw a full gasp of surprise—or reengage his sword.

"The differences between us," Gawain whispered into the ear of the dying man.

Severe lack of emotion and abundance of wit.

What Gawain possessed and most did not.

With a quick jerk, Gawain freed his sword. As the body crumpled to the ground, he swiped both sides of his weapon on the cleanest patch of the soldier's woolen tunic. He believed in letting fallen men keep their blood. *Off my sword.*

English! The revelation of how far and wide their exposure had traveled still stunned him.

No time! He charged back toward the footpath and raced on.

After another few hundred yards, the clear sounds of combat filtered into the dense forest: the clatter of weapons, shouts and grunts from men.

Seconds later, he burst upon a greater battle. Or what little remained of it.

His brethren carved and sliced through their own tenacious dark-garbed attackers. One Brodie to five English. But the last of their foe fell in rapid succession, one after the other, none prepared for the skill of the unique clan of Highlanders.

With no immediate threat left to eliminate, Gawain sheathed his weapon.

A second strange thunder boomed through his chest.

And its fading vibration carried the aftertaste of something imminent...*weighty*. As if an event of great import was about to transpire. *Involving me?* Or the clan.

Dismayed by the inexplicable and unnerving sensation,

Gawain stared toward the western horizon as a fiery sun dipped below jagged mountain peaks.

Two warhorses suddenly appeared below his line of vision, one snow white, the other coal black. Both materialized seemingly from nowhere. And knowing their riders as Gawain did, they likely had.

Another powerful vibration reverberated through Gawain's chest so hard, he stifled the urge to cough as his family approached.

Astride the white mare was Isobel Brodie with her long blond hair flying back in the wind. Clad in her custom deerskin hunting outfit, she braced her toddler son between her arms.

On the black stallion rode Iain, Isobel's husband, Gawain's older brother, and Laird of Clan Brodie. He cradled their lad's twin sister with a father's protective hand.

Clutched in Iain's other hand was a magickal box whose surface sparkled even in gloaming's waning light.

Yet that box had *never* left Brodie Castle.

Not in all the years of Gawain's life.

Nor in any of the legendary tales of generations past.

An unmistakable sense of foreboding washed over him as his fellow warriors gathered to watch their leader and kin draw near.

"*All* approach the battlefront?" their commander, Robert, inquired to his right.

"With the wee ones?" Duncan asked at his left.

The warriors were part of Iain's elite guardsmen. Twelve in total. Closer than brothers.

"Nay." Naught was as it seemed. A great change had begun. Those facts rang true with every heavy beat of his heart. And he'd somehow landed in the center of its shifting tides. "They'll be but a moment," he murmured.

Even if Gawain failed to comprehend *how* he knew what was about to transpire, he sensed why they'd come.

Fate had descended upon him. Though the circumstance made little sense.

"I'll not take your place!" Gawain objected to the notion. The magickal box may as well have been scepter, orb, and crown. For of the many powers it wielded, foremost among them had long been to ordain the next Brodie male as chieftain of their clan.

"*Aye*, you will." Iain lifted the hallowed box high, reaching back.

"You remain hale and whole." Fit to rule. No reason to shift the obligation.

"We've no time to explain." Isobel tightened her legs to bring her mount alongside Iain's as she glanced at her husband. "Danger abounds. And we've been summoned"— at the last word, she directed Gawain a pointed look, heavy with meaning—"*away*."

Gawain sighed. *Away through* time itself. *No explanation needed.*

A strange feeling quivered in his gut. Akin to uncertainty. And a more familiar one: dread. Of the unknown. Of the burden of a reign he had never expected to shoulder.

The obsessive focus of battle had served him well all his life, had helped him overcome childhood demons. Even to the detriment of relations with close family. Namely his sister, Brigid, who he'd wrongly blamed for the cause of those demons so long ago. But Gawain had already come to accept how he'd done Brigid a grave disservice and labored to make amends.

Of late, he'd grown more noble. Worthy of the reign.

And his brother well knew it.

"'Tis the way of it," Iain bellowed for all the guardsmen to hear in witness of the historic moment. "You'll lead the clan through."

"*Aye.*" Gawain gave a clipped nod to his brother in dutiful acceptance of the role.

Iain dipped his chin with satisfaction, punched his arm forward, and released his grip.

The box arced through the air.

With narrowed eyes, Gawain thrust his hands up to catch it.

Yet at the exact moment his fingertips made contact with its cool metal sides, several monumental events happened at once, in plain sight of their guardsmen.

A bright bolt of lightning shot from ground to sky with a true boom of thunder.

Isobel touched a hand to Iain's shoulder and Clan Brodie's former ruling family vanished, warhorses and all.

Heat sparked from the box to his fingers and flashed through his entire body.

And a raven-haired woman appeared out of thin air. Vibrant blue eyes stared straight at him. Her slender hand rested atop the box.

"*Nay!*" Gawain growled, furious.

In his disgruntled shock of becoming laird, he'd forgotten the *other* burden the ancient box bestowed.

A soul mate.

Enjoy the rest of the adventure...
Found in Flame and Moonlight

ABOUT THE AUTHOR

Kat Bastion won several awards for her bestselling debut novel *Forged in Dreams and Magick*.

Kat & Stone Bastion's bestselling first novel *No Weddings* and the No Weddings series were named Best of 2014 by multiple romance review blogs.

When not defining love and redemption through scribed words, they enjoy hiking in vivid wildflower deserts, ancient tropical forests, and historic urban jungles.

Join our Bastion Family Adventurers!

Be in the know with preorder alerts, exclusive bonus gifts, and occasional free stories:

https://www.katbastion.com/email-subscription/

Let's be social...

f facebook.com/KatANDStoneBastion

twitter.com/KatBastion

a amazon.com/Kat-Bastion/e/B00FBL9PZ4

g goodreads.com/KatBastion

BB bookbub.com/authors/kat-bastion

www.ingramcontent.com/pod-product-compliance
Lightning Source LLC
Chambersburg PA
CBHW052007020726
47501CB00004B/1043